Heartwood Hotel

Home Again

Kallie George

illustrated by
Stephanie Graegin

LITTLE, BROWN AND COMPANY
NEW YORK BOSTON

To my growing family
—k.g.

For Gloria
—s.g.

Text copyright © 2018 by Kallie George
Illustrations copyright © 2018 by Stephanie Graegin

Cover art copyright © 2018 by Stephanie Graegin. Cover copyright © 2018 by Hachette Book Group, Inc.

Little, Brown and Company
Hachette Book Group
1290 Avenue of the Americas, New York, NY 10104
Visit us at LBYR.com

Originally published in hardcover, trade paperback, and ebook by Disney • Hyperion, an imprint of Disney Publishing Group, in July 2018
First Edition: July 2018

Little, Brown and Company is a division of Hachette Book Group, Inc. The Little, Brown name and logo are trademarks of Hachette Book Group, Inc.

The publisher is not responsible for websites (or their content) that are not owned by the publisher.

Library of Congress Cataloging-in-Publication Data
Names: George, Kallie, author. • Graegin, Stephanie, illustrator.
Title: Home again / by Kallie George ; illustrated by Stephanie Graegin.
Description: First edition. • Los Angeles : New York : Disney-Hyperion, 2018. • Series: Heartwood Hotel ; 4 • Summary: "Summer has come to Fernwood Forest, and the staff of the Heartwood Hotel must trust each other as they contend with their biggest challenge yet"—Provided by publisher.
Identifiers: LCCN 2017056151• ISBN 9781484732366 (hardback) • ISBN 1484732367 (hardcover)
Subjects: • CYAC: Hotels, motels, etc.—Fiction. • Forest animals—Fiction. • Summer—Fiction. Forest fires—Fiction. • Weddings—Fiction. • BISAC: JUVENILE FICTION / Animals / Mice, Hamsters, Guinea Pigs, etc. • JUVENILE FICTION / Nature & the Natural World / General (see also headings under Animals). • JUVENILE FICTION / Family / Alternative Family.
Classification: LCC PZ7.G293326 Hom 2018 • DDC [Fic]—dc23
LC record available at https://lccn.loc.gov/2017056151

ISBNs: 978-1-484-73236-6 (hardcover), 978-1-484-74680-6 (pbk.), 978-1-484-74739-1 (ebook)

Printed in the United States of America

LSC-C

Printing 4, 2020

Contents

THE DRESS DISASTER

There was no place like the Heartwood Hotel. It was the biggest tree in the whole of Fernwood Forest. At one end lay the Foothills, at the other the village, and in the very center grew the grand hotel, with the stream winding its way around it like a long curly whisker. Everyone loved the Heartwood—especially in the summertime. Mostly it was a resting spot for animals, but for staff, like Mona the maid, it was home.

A very poky home!

Sunshine and spines filled the hotel as everyone, staff and guests alike, prepared for a porcupine wedding. Not just any porcupines—Ms. Prickles, the cook, was marrying Mr. Quillson, a former guest who had swept her off her paws.

Today was the big day. Mona and her best friend, Tilly the squirrel, had been excused from their maid duties. They were in Mona's room getting dressed up. Tilly could be a bit of a grump, but even *she* couldn't be grumpy when they put on new heart-patterned dresses instead of their aprons, then ran upstairs to help the bride get ready.

They found Ms. Prickles tucked in a corner of the salon on the second floor. The room was packed quill-to-quill with her porcupine relatives primping and preparing. It was almost impossible to move without being poked. Luckily, the salon was run by a possum who could hang from the ceiling by his tail.

That's what he was doing now, busily shining quills upside down. Mona had never been properly introduced. Perkins liked to keep to himself. And it was no surprise, considering how bossy everyone seemed.

"Make sure you cover up my gray ones with soot polish," an old porcupine ordered the possum.

"Am I finished sitting under the fur-fluffer?" asked another. "It's hot enough in here without *added* heat. And besides, I don't even HAVE fur!"

It *was* very hot. The whole summer had been. Anxious guests were beginning to lose their tempers.

"Don't tug so hard!" complained the old porcupine.

WHISH!

One of her quills flew out and stuck in the ceiling, narrowly missing the possum and drawing everyone's attention. Perkins gave Mona a wide-eyed look.

Mona winced. Being the smallest of the staff, she had managed so far to avoid being poked.

But not Tilly. She'd been poked twice. Make that *three* times. . . .

"Ouch!" Tilly cried. "Mona, *you* do it!" She handed Mona the wedding dress.

As Tilly soothed her sore side, Mona tugged the dress over Ms. Prickles's spines. Two quills ripped through the fabric.

"This will never do!" Ms. Prickles moaned.

Mona was about to agree, when she realized the porcupine wasn't talking about her dress. She was consulting a list clutched in her paw. "If one more guest shows up, I don't know what will happen!" she said under her breath.

"But I thought everyone had arrived," said Mona.

"*As if,*" said Tilly, rolling her eyes.

"More keep coming!" replied Ms. Prickles. "I wish weddings weren't so full of surprises. I prefer my seedcakes stacked where I can see them. I can't count the number of aunts and uncles and cousins here." She glanced around the room, then said, in a hush, "And you'd think, with so many relatives, *one* of them would be able to cook." She sighed. "My aunt can barely boil a barley seed, and *she's* in charge of the cake. Goodness knows what will happen!"

Truthfully, Mona couldn't imagine anything better than having a big party with so many relatives. This was the first wedding she'd ever attended. But Tilly, who had overseen a number of them at the hotel, said that wedding parties were weird. "You never know *who* might start crying."

Indeed, it looked like Ms. Prickles might right now.

"Don't worry," Mona said. Usually Ms. Prickles was the voice of comfort. "Let's get you dressed."

Together, she and Tilly tugged on the dress. *RIIIP!* It split right in half. Just as Ms. Prickles burst into tears, Henry popped his head into the salon. "There you are!" he cried.

Henry was Tilly's younger brother and also a bellhop at the hotel. He scurried around the porcupines to get to Mona and Tilly. He got poked a few times but didn't seem to mind. Mona could tell he was excited because his red tail was puffed up as big as his body.

"Guess what! Guess what!" He didn't wait for them to answer. "Someone's here!"

Ms. Prickles's sobs grew louder. "Another guest?" she cried.

"Another porcupine?" groaned Tilly.

Henry nodded his head vigorously—then shook it. "Yes. No. I mean . . . it is a guest. But it isn't a porcupine." Henry took a deep breath. "And she isn't here to see you, Ms. Prickles." He pointed at Mona. "She's here for you!"

Mona couldn't believe it. Now that *was* a surprise!

The Mysterious Mouse

Who could be waiting for me? Mona wondered as she hurried down the staircase that circled the center of the tree, from the star-gazing balcony at the tip-top to the hibernation suites in the deep dirt. The majestic old oak could accommodate all types of guests, from feathered to furred.

Still, Mona wasn't expecting a visitor of any kind. She didn't *know* anyone, other than the staff and a few guests she'd made friends with.

When she reached the lobby, she paused. It was just as full of porcupines as the salon! The poky guests were hustling and bustling about, paws full of packages and decorations.

The whole lobby was decorated for the wedding. Prickly purple thistles were strung along the front desk. Blue ones hung above the front door. Thistles were even blooming in the fireplace. Mr. Heartwood had given strict orders not to light any fires, as they could be dangerous during hot, dry summers. (Only the kitchen was allowed one, but even so, the menu had been featuring mostly salads.) So the fireplace was filled with a giant bouquet of flame-colored thistles instead. And there, in front, stood a guest who was definitely *not* a porcupine.

It was a mouse!

In all the months that Mona had worked at the Heartwood—three whole seasons—she had never encountered another mouse. Her parents had stayed there long ago. Her dad had even carved the

heart on the front door. But Mona had yet to meet one of her own kind at the grand hotel. Why was a mouse here? To meet *her*? Did it have something to do with her parents?

The new arrival wore a large straw hat with a fancy pink bow on the back. In one paw she clutched a suitcase made from a box that said MATCHES. Mona had never seen a suitcase like that before. Tucked under the mouse's arm was a rolled-up *Pinecone Press*. She was staring at the sign above the fireplace mantel: WE LIVE BY "PROTECT AND RESPECT," NOT BY "TOOTH AND CLAW," and she was nodding.

"That's our motto," said Mona, coming up behind her. "I was told you were looking for me?"

The mouse turned and, upon seeing Mona, smiled. Mona was sure she'd never met the mouse before, yet something about her seemed familiar. She was much older than Mona. Her fur was graying but still glossy, and her eyes were kind. She had white gloves on, and around her neck hung a little seed, carved into a heart. Her jacket was embroidered with the letters IB. Mona didn't know what it stood for, but the effect was very stylish. Mona was glad she was dressed up, too.

"Mercy me, you must be Mona," said the mouse, in a slow, sweet voice, putting down the suitcase and pulling off a glove. She extended her paw. "I've heard all about you."

"You . . . you have?" stammered Mona, shaking the mouse's paw.

"Yes." The mouse studied Mona from nose to tail. "I . . . well . . ." For a moment, she seemed lost for words, then at last she said, "You look so . . . so young. I expected . . . But no, of course you're young," hurried the mouse. "Were you always a maid?"

"No, actually, I started working at the hotel only a year ago," said Mona.

"Oh, and you were living with your parents before that?"

"No," Mona said again, feeling a little confused by the questions. "My parents . . . they died a long time ago. I don't have any family."

The mouse touched her necklace. "Oh, sugar, I am . . . so sorry," she said. She really meant it. Mona could tell.

"It's okay. You didn't know," said Mona. "I have a great home now here at the Heartwood."

The mouse nodded. "Word has it, you are a marvelous maid."

Mona blushed. "But . . . who are you?"

"My name is Strawberry," the mouse replied. "I'm from the Inn Between."

"The Inn Between?" questioned Mona.

"Yes. You haven't heard of us?" Strawberry looked disappointed.

"Of course we have!" burst a voice. Gilles, the front-desk lizard, popped out from between two porcupines and straightened his green bow tie. "The Inn Between is only *the* best hotel for mice and small creatures in the village! What a wonderful idea, to repurpose the in-between floors of a house and turn them into a specialty hotel. Mind you, I must say I'd be quite concerned about being sighted living amongst the large."

"I make sure our staff are very well-trained—and very careful," said Strawberry.

"What a pleasure to meet one of the owners. Is it true you have over a dozen of the best mice maids working for you? So, so impressive." Gilles's tongue flicked in and out.

Now it was Strawberry's turn to blush. "Yes, well, I actually thought *all* the best mice maids worked for me, which is why I was surprised to hear about Mona."

"*Tsk-tsk*, no getting any ideas," said Gilles, giving Mona's shoulder a protective pat. "This is one of our star employees. We're not letting you steal her away."

Mona felt her cheeks grow warm again, but she

was very glad Gilles had said it and she didn't have to. She didn't want to go anywhere! She loved the Heartwood.

"Oh, mercy me, of course not," said Strawberry. "I just wanted to meet her and see your lovely hotel. I have some vacation time, and I've been meaning to visit, though I don't like to travel outside the village. The forest is a touch frightening."

Mona didn't think it was so scary, especially in the bright, warm summer, but she'd grown up in Fernwood.

Strawberry went on, "The Inn Between would so love a review in the *Pinecone Press*, and I was hoping to get some ideas from the Heartwood—"

Gilles frowned.

Strawberry quickly added, "Only ideas, of course. Perhaps Mona could show me around, as long as Mr. Heartwood doesn't mind?"

Mona knew that Mr. Heartwood liked to help other hotels. Recently, he'd helped his friend

Benjamin the beaver open the Beaver Lodge, a hotel for water animals.

"I'd love to, except . . ." started Mona.

"Except it's our cook's wedding today," interrupted Gilles, "and the celebration is being held at the Heartwood. A cook marrying a guest—highly unusual—but who's to stop true love? It's the biggest wedding we've ever hosted, and Mr. Heartwood is busy in the garden setting up. I must excuse myself, too. You know how it is. Mona can help you check in." With that, Gilles gave a bow, and hurried off to stop a young porcupette, who had gotten her paws on a guest book—and a pawful of inky pens.

"Please, come this way," said Mona to Strawberry. "I'll get you your key. And then I'll have to excuse myself, too. I need to help the bride with her dress. It's a bit of an emergency." Mona paused. "You see, there's a . . ."

"FIRE!" came a cry. *"FIIIIIIIIIIIRE!"*

THE CAKE CATASTROPHE

"*FIIIIIIIIIIIIRE!*" the cry came again.

Through the crowd of porcupines pushed another porcupine, whom Mona recognized. It was Ms. Prickles's Uncle Bristle. All his quills were sticking straight up.

Mona's fur stuck straight up, too. Fire?! This was exactly what Mr. Heartwood—what everyone—feared most.

But when she got a better look at Uncle Bristle and noticed that he was covered in flour and wearing Ms. Prickles's apron, Mona knew it wasn't a forest fire.

"The wedding cake!" she cried.

Immediately, Mona rushed to the stairs, weaving between perplexed porcupines. With every step down toward the kitchen, the smell of smoke grew stronger. Uncle Bristle hurried close behind her.

Mona stepped into the kitchen and—*POOF!*—into a billowing cloud of smoke.

It was coming from the fireplace at the back. Mona could make out another porcupine there, Ms. Prickles's Auntie Barb. She was wearing one oven mitt on her head and flapping the smoke away with

another. Didn't she know oven mitts weren't hats? And they weren't for fanning smoke either! Fanning a fire made it grow!

Mona peered through the haze, searching for something to put out the flames. The kitchen was such a mess it was hard to find anything. The big table, where the staff shared their meals, was covered in acorn flour, cake batter, and pawprints. Spoons and seeds were scattered across the floor. Pots and pans piled up in the shell sink. At last, Mona spied a dish full of dirty water. Grabbing it, she ran to the fireplace and tossed the water on the flames.

SPLASH!

SIZZLE!

POOOOOF!

An even greater cloud of smoke filled the air.

Mona held her breath and squinted her eyes as everyone disappeared from view.

Slowly, the smoke cleared. To Mona's great relief, the flames were gone.

"Oh, good!" she said.

"Oh no!" shrieked Auntie Barb, whose voice was as sharp as her name.

"But look! The fire's out," said Mona. "It's okay."

"It's not okay!" the porcupine shrieked even louder.

She pointed to the baking shelf. There, above the coals, looking very much like a big lump of coal itself, was the wedding cake.

"But . . . but I saved us . . ." stammered Mona. "The kitchen could have caught fire. The cake was burning."

"It was SUPPOSED to burn," replied Auntie Barb. "It was going to be a *burnt* cake!"

"Don't you mean . . . *Bundt* cake?" asked Mona, who remembered Ms. Prickles once making a strange cake that looked a little like a nest.

"Yes, burnt!" said Auntie Barb. "The fire was on purpose. Uncle Bristle just overreacted. He doesn't appreciate my cooking. Nobody does! Now it's ruined!" The quills on her head poked right through the oven mitt.

"Ruined?" a voice snipped back. Mrs. Higgins, the hedgehog housekeeper and sternest of the staff, strode into the room. "Mona saved you from burning down the entire hotel. What on earth were you thinking? This is the dry season. We must be *extra* careful not to start any fires." Mrs. Higgins crossed her arms.

"But we had to bake a cake," said Auntie Barb.

"Bake, yes—burn, no!" scolded Mrs. Higgins.

"Burn, bake . . . Everyone's a critic!" cried Auntie Barb, bursting into tears. "I've had enough." With difficulty, she pulled off the punctured oven mitt. She threw it on the table and stormed out of the room, Uncle Bristle following dutifully behind her.

"Suit yourselves," Mrs. Higgins called after them, adding, under her breath, "I've never SEEN such prickly porcupines."

"But, Mrs. Higgins, the cake! Who will bake it?" said Mona.

Mrs. Higgins looked a little worried. "Yes, well . . ."

"Maybe I can," came a voice.

In the doorway stood a mouse wearing a big hat. Strawberry! She seemed hesitant to come in. "I may be on holiday, but I was wondering if you could use a spare pair of paws? At the Inn Between, I'm always chasing one disaster after another. I'm especially good in the kitchen."

"The Inn Between?" said Mrs. Higgins. "That's a fine establishment. . . . But you're a guest. We couldn't possibly . . ." Then, to Mona's surprise, Mrs. Higgins shook her head. "It's too late for proper protocol. The cake should have been done hours ago. Are you sure?"

The mouse nodded.

Mona smiled.

"Very well. Come in, come in. Mona, show

her around the kitchen," directed Mrs. Higgins. "Weddings," she sighed, as she left. "I am glad Mr. Higgins and I eloped. It really is the *sensible* way of doing things."

Strawberry took off her hat, and Mona found her an apron, and one for herself, too. Then, together, they set to work.

Mona had only helped in the kitchen once before, making tiny treats for insects. But she was good at cleaning—and fetching. She scurried back and forth, bringing acorn flour from the storage room, freshly picked berries from upstairs, and honey from the house hive, run by Captain Ruby, who preferred being called Captain to Queen.

Strawberry, meanwhile, measured and stirred.

After Mona had fetched all the ingredients, she cleaned. As she swept the floor with her upside-down dandelion broom, she told Strawberry a bit about the Heartwood. Soon the kitchen was just how Ms. Prickles liked it—spick-and-span. And it smelled right again, too. Rich and nutty and sweet. The cake was on the baking shelf, and Strawberry was watching it closely.

"It looks perfect," said Mona.

"It's my specialty, Very Berry Shortcake," said Strawberry. "Though I don't make it much. Most of our food is collected from the floors."

"Collected?"

"Yes. Staff take turns finding and picking up crumbs from under tables and chairs. Then the sorters in the kitchen organize the crumbs. And our cook adds toppings—like cinnamon and sugar. But I prefer proper baking. I've always been good with my paws."

Good with her paws? That was exactly what Mona had heard others say about her mom, and it gave her a strange, happy shiver.

"Kitchens are my favorite spot," continued Strawberry.

"Mine too," said Mona. She'd met Tilly in

 24

this kitchen, and celebrated her first St. Slumber's Supper here as well.

"They're so cozy and safe. At least . . ." Strawberry gave a pointed glance at Aunt Barb's cake. "At least at the Inn Between."

Mona and Strawberry both laughed.

Strawberry wiggled her whiskers. "Ah. There. It's ready. Whiskers curl when the cake is baked."

She put on the oven mitt without holes and lifted the cake from the baking shelf. Mona quickly picked up Strawberry's hat off the table to make room for it. The cake looked beautiful, like a tiny golden moon.

After letting it sit a moment, Strawberry carefully cut it into the shape of a heart. She scooped up the trimmings and handed one to Mona.

"And now for the best part. Go on, sugar, take a bite."

Mona did. Strawberry and honey melted on her tongue. It was delicious.

"A quick cool, a bit of cream, and it will be ready," said Strawberry. "We can't keep the bride waiting on her special day."

The bride!

All at once, Mona remembered Ms. Prickles and her dress. She couldn't believe she'd forgotten! Tilly wasn't very good with problem-solving. She was probably still scrambling to find a replacement. There were plenty of porcupines there, but none of them would have brought a wedding dress. What could Mona do? She glanced at the hat in her paw. The big bow bobbed merrily.

Maybe they didn't need another dress.

Mona had an idea.

STRAWBERRY STAYS

The salon was empty now, except for a distressed porcupine and a very grumpy Tilly. "Where WERE you?" Tilly exclaimed the moment Mona returned. "I borrowed three different dresses from three different guests, and look!" said the squirrel, pointing to a stack of shredded fabric on the floor.

"I'm sorry," said Mona. "There was a small problem. But everything's fixed."

"Not *everything*!" cried her friend. "What about the dress!"

"About that," said Mona, "I think I know what to do."

The music had just started when Mona, Tilly, and Ms. Prickles arrived in the courtyard. Blackberry and raspberry vines were woven into a heart-shaped arbor, and pots of thistles lined the mossy aisle.

As the music grew louder, Mona and Tilly joined the rest of the staff, slipping onto mushroom-cap chairs. Mona had never seen all the staff so dressed

up. Mr. Heartwood was wearing a top hat, Mrs. Higgins had a lace handkerchief, and Mr. Higgins sported an extra blossom pinned on his prickles.

"Ooh!" the crowd gasped as Ms. Prickles made her way down the aisle. She wasn't wearing a wedding dress. She wasn't wearing a dress at all. Instead, bows bobbed from her quills in a bouquet of bright colors. Mona's paws were still sore from tying them all. But it was worth it.

Ms. Prickles looked spectacular—or so Mona

thought. But Mr. Quillson started crying at the sight of her. "Good," whispered Tilly, much to Mona's surprise. "The groom is *supposed* to cry."

Weddings really are weird, Mona thought.

But also wonderful! Everyone cheered when the little porcupette made it down the aisle without dropping the rings hanging off his quills. Everyone cheered again when the two porcupines kissed— except for Henry, who looked away, embarrassed. But he cheered extra loudly when it was time to eat cake—and made sure he was first in line.

All the guests (and staff, too) loved Strawberry's Very Berry Shortcake. In fact, Mrs. Prickles, upon taking a bite, was so impressed she said, "Now, this is who should take my place while I'm on my honeymoon!"

Mona couldn't agree more.

"If you need me . . ." said Strawberry, blushing. "Only for a few weeks, though—while my holiday lasts."

"It's settled, then," said Mr. Heartwood, stepping forward, presenting his plate for a second slice. "A cook to stay while Ms. Pr—*Mrs.* Prickles is away. What splendid luck!"

And then . . . even more luck. It began to rain! A summer shower played like music across Fernwood Forest, refreshing the whole earth.

Mona ducked under a tall toadstool and watched as everyone, laughing, hurried for shelter, too. The newlywed couple, Henry and Tilly, and all the porcupine relatives, from porcupettes to great-grandparents. What a lot of families!

Mona smiled and finished her cake—just in time. Tilly ducked under the toadstool. But she wasn't after Mona's cake. She was there to grump, "Henry wants to play in the puddles. He better not splash anyone—especially not that fancy new mouse!"

She glanced at Strawberry,

who was under the arbor, pinned between two por-cupines. "Why would she want to work here, as a cook, when she's supposed to be on vacation? Who wants to work on vacation?!"

"Strawberry does," replied Mona. "She's here to learn about the Heartwood to help her hotel, the Inn Between."

"The Inn Between?" said Tilly. "All the best mouse maids work there. Except for you." Tilly raised her eyebrows. "Do you think she's here to steal you away?"

Mona's whiskers twitched. "That's exactly what Gilles said. But I don't think so." Strawberry didn't seem like the stealing sort.

Tilly nodded and glanced at Strawberry again. "You know, she looks a bit like you, Mona. Do you think she might be a . . ."

"A relative?" whispered Mona. The thought was sweeter than any piece of cake. She had every-thing else: a wonderful home, plenty of food, and a best friend—grumpy though she was. But she didn't have any real family.

She remembered the questions Strawberry had asked, and how she was good with her paws. But Mona shook her head. "No, she would have told me."

Before Tilly could reply, a flash came from the sky, lighting up the trees in the distance, like the flicker of a thousand fireflies. Mona gasped. It seemed like a sign.

But of what, the sky wouldn't share.

Back inside, the thought of a sign soon slipped Mona's mind as the band began to play.

"Put your prickly paw in mine.
You're my poky-woky porcupine."

Mona stayed up very late, dancing with Tilly till her paws hurt. She kept stealing glances at Strawberry, trying hard to see any resemblance. Both their noses *were* extra pointy. . . .

Mr. Heartwood was the only one who didn't dance, sitting on a root, sipping chilled honey. "An old badger like me is content with his tree," he said. But he did join in for one last picture. In fact, it was his idea. "One of us all to put on the wall," he said. Nobody needed to be told where to stand. All the staff gathered around him.

"Very good, very good," said the Official Memory Maker, a millipede, whose arms and legs were already busy drawing. "Your portrait will only take a moment."

"Stop squirming, Henry!" said Tilly.

"I'm not! I'm trying to tell you Francis is here!"

And he was! When the picture was done, it was time for the prickly pair to head off on their honeymoon, in a wagon pulled by Francis the deer.

Mona stared at the ribbons on the back of the wagon until they were whisker-thin. She would miss Mrs. Prickles.

Mr. Heartwood must have read her mind, since

 34

he placed a heavy paw on her shoulder. "There, there, Miss Mouse. Mrs. Prickles will be back soon," he said. "And Mr. Quillson will fit in nicely at the Heartwood. After all, he is a doctor, and we certainly could use a physician here. . . ." He gave Mona a teasing look. She *had* gotten into a lot of scrapes over the seasons. "With a wedding, a family grows. In how many ways, nobody knows," Mr. Heartwood added.

Mona was sure he meant Mr. Quillson, but . . . She glanced over at Strawberry, who was cleaning up, and felt hope flutter in her chest, like a small bright ribbon.

Harmony the Hummingbird

Mona didn't go to bed until the sun was almost up. And she wasn't the only one. When she arrived in the kitchen in the morning, still sleepy, she found most of the staff groggy-eyed, some even wearing their pajamas. Only Strawberry was bright, bustling about, ready with a delicious breakfast for them all—little huckleberry pancakes in the shape of flowers and stars. She placed a special one, shaped like a heart, in front of Mona. "There you go, sugar."

"See," whispered Tilly, giving Mona a nudge. "I told you."

Mona *did* wonder. But it was just a pancake, not proof.

The next few days were busy tidying up from the wedding and checking out a preponderance of porcupines.

When at last things settled, Mona tried to find time alone with Strawberry to learn more about her. But there was always someone else in the kitchen: Henry wanting more of Strawberry's Very Berry Shortcake; Gilles gasping over the revelation that the famous opera star Havarti Provolone had stayed at the Inn Between; Mrs. Higgins discussing the merits of daily schedules with her.

Somehow Strawberry also found time to put her own touches on the kitchen—not to change it at all, but to add a few fancy details Mona knew Mrs. Prickles would love. Like fresh flowers on the table every morning, and spiderweb lace around their place mats.

Yes, everyone liked Strawberry. Which was a good thing, decided Mona, especially if they were related.

It was hard not to look for more signs. Mona had spent all spring trying to find even one guest-book entry written by her parents. Although she hadn't found any, there was one clue: that she had relatives. Strawberry couldn't be a cousin. She was too old. She could be an aunt, though . . .

Every morning at breakfast, Mona noticed how Strawberry tested her hot honey with a whisker, just the way she did. But maybe there were some things that all mice did the same? Mona didn't know. She had never spent any time around other mice.

One morning, she finally caught Strawberry alone. The mouse was busy writing a letter. Mona was wondering whether to interrupt her when Strawberry murmured her name.

"Mona . . ."

"Yes?" said Mona.

Strawberry looked up. "Oh, sugar. I didn't realize you were here."

Mona was confused. Hadn't Strawberry just said her name?

Strawberry didn't explain. Instead, she quickly rolled up the paper, a little piece of bark, and tied string around it. "I have a letter that needs to be sent to the Inn Between. Do you know where I should put it?"

"The messenger jay picks up the post from the mailbox, right after breakfast," said Mona.

"Mercy me," said Strawberry, "I'm just in time. I haven't started heating up the honey, and you know how much Mr. Heartwood needs his cup of hot honey in the morning. Could you post it, sugar?"

"Of course," said Mona. "Maybe after we could . . ."

"Spend a little time together." Strawberry smiled warmly.

Mona took the letter and hurried out of the kitchen. As she scurried up the stairs, she began to wonder what was in the note. She was tempted to peek, but she knew how wrong that was. You weren't supposed to read someone else's mail. Ever. Still, the bark seemed to burn in her paw, and she kept stealing glances down at it, all the way across the lobby, out the door, until—*WHOOMP*—she collided with Mr. Heartwood.

The letter flew out of Mona's paw. The string

popped off and the bark unrolled on the mossy ground. She scrambled to pick it up, but not before her eye caught some of the words, written in berry ink:

I'm sure it's Mona. She's the one,

Mona's heart caught in her throat. *She's the one?* What did that mean?

"Miss Mouse, are you okay?" asked Mr. Heartwood.

Mona quickly collected Strawberry's letter and looked up at the stately badger. He was wearing his night-robe, but his tie was already fastened around his neck. He held a letter in his paw, too.

"Yes. . . . I have a letter for the jay, from Strawberry." Mona retied the string around it, her heart pounding.

Mr. Heartwood frowned. "And I have mail as well, for my friend Benjamin, but we have a bit of a problem."

"What problem?" asked Mona.

Mr. Heartwood pointed at the mailbox slightly above his head. Sunshine had begun to creep through the canopy, lighting up the box. The box was made from a hollowed-out burl that had a slot for putting mail in and a little door, which only the jay could open, for getting it back out. The box seemed to be quivering.

"The messenger is in the mailbox. I don't know what happened," said Mr. Heartwood. "I merely asked what good news she could share, and now she's hiding up in there!"

"In *there?*" said Mona. She knew the size of most of the jays. "How does she even fit?"

"It's not a jay, but a hummingbird," said Mr. Heartwood, pulling out his handkerchief and mopping his brow. "A small one—smaller than you. I am not sure what to do. I think she might be crying."

Crying?

"What do you think startled her so?" Mr. Heartwood continued.

"I don't know," said Mona, "but I can find out."

After all, she was almost as small as a hummingbird. She could fit in the mailbox, too.

"Thank you, Miss Mouse," said Mr. Heartwood.

Mona tucked Strawberry's letter in her apron pocket and, with a boost from Mr. Heartwood, scrambled onto the perch that stuck out just below the mailbox. The perch was wide but slippery, worn smooth from so many claws landing on it  over the years. Carefully Mona inched her way to the slot and squirmed her way in.

It took Mona's eyes a moment to adjust to the darkness. When they did, she could see, hidden in the hollow beside a bundle of mail, a tiny bird, so frightened even her long beak was trembling. The bird's shiny black eyes widened when she saw Mona.

"Are you okay?" asked Mona gently.

The hummingbird didn't reply.

"I'm Mona, a maid at the Heartwood," Mona continued. "Mr. Heartwood sent me up here to check on you. I've never seen a messenger *hummingbird* before. You must be very special."

Still the hummingbird didn't reply.

"Don't you want to share your news?"

At last the little bird spoke. Her words came out all in a rush. "No-I-don't-That's-the-problem." Her breath smelled sweet, like nectar.

"Would you say that again, please?" asked Mona as politely as she could.

"No, I don't," said the hummingbird again, a little bit slower, but still so fast Mona had to listen closely to understand. Before Mona could ask why not, the hummingbird went on, faster again, like a hum. "I-always-wanted-to-be-a-messenger-Hummingbirds-are-usually-too-small-for-all-the-letters-But-I-trained-myself-I-strengthened-my-wings-Just-because-you-might-be-small-doesn't-mean-you-can't-do-it."

Mona nodded. That she understood, even if it was said at the speed of lightning.

"I-like-making-animals-happy-That's-why-my-parents-named-me-Harmony-I-wanted-to-be-a-messenger-to-bring-good-news-to-animals-Wedding-invitations-birthday-announcements-lost-family-found . . ."

Lost family found. That's what Mona hoped Strawberry's letter was about. "I have good news for you to bring," said Mona. "At least, I think it is . . ."

"You do?" said Harmony, slowing down in amazement.

 45

Mona pulled out Strawberry's letter from her apron pocket. The happy bow around the letter seemed to prove it. Harmony took it carefully.

"But-I-don't-have-good-news-to-give-back," said the bird.

"That's okay," said Mona. "There's always some good news and some bad news. That's what makes the good news good," she added.

"Really?"

Mona nodded.

She hadn't thought of it before, but it was true. There had been many scary times at the Heartwood, but there had been the best moments, too. "Without the bad, how would you even know what *was* good?"

"I . . . suppose," said Harmony, looking brighter, but only for a moment. Her voice wavered as she went on, "My-bad-news-it's-*really*-bad." She gulped.

Mona gulped, too. Really bad news? Her heart started to hum, quick as Harmony's voice. "What is it?" she asked. "Mr. Heartwood *needs* to know. Trust me, Harmony. Even if he's upset, it won't be at you."

"It's-a-fire," whispered Harmony. She took a breath and said slowly, "There's a fire in Fernwood."

A Fortunate Find

"A fire? How? When? Where?" said Mr. Heartwood.

The sunlight was bright now, shining through the canopy and lighting the forest floor in yellow stripes, like flames. Harmony had left the mailbox and was now hovering in front of the badger, with Mona nearby.

The hummingbird looked at her nervously. The news was worse than Mona could have imagined.

Still . . . "Go on," she said, as encouragingly as she could.

"It-was-the-storm-the-lightning," said Harmony in a rush.

The lightning, at the wedding! Mona remembered how pretty it had been. Pretty—and terrible! It must have hit a tree and set it alight. Mona's fur stood on end, like she had been struck by lightning herself.

"But where? Where is it?" said Mr. Heartwood.

"In-the-far-part-of-Fernwood-The-Foothills," the hummingbird said.

Mr. Heartwood seemed to breathe easier. And that made Mona feel better. "There is much forest between there and the Heartwood. The weather will change and rains will come. But to be safe, we must alert everyone."

Before Mr. Heartwood could ask, Harmony said, to Mona's surprise: "I'll do it. I'm the messenger."

"No, no," said Mr. Heartwood stoutly. "Leave it to me. You go on. Alert others of the danger that's here. It *is* grave danger, be it far or near. Thank you, Miss Hummingbird."

Harmony's black eyes glittered with purpose. With the bundle of mail tucked in the bag slung across her chest, she flew off into the morning.

"Fire?"

"Fire!"

"FIRE!"

The word crackled across the ballroom. Mr.

Heartwood and Mona had gathered the guests and staff there to tell them the news. Breakfast—daisy-leaf doughnuts—lay abandoned in the dining room.

"In the Foothills? I have a brother there!" said a nervous rabbit.

"Do you know how quickly it's spreading?" asked a butterfly.

Before the meeting had ended, there was already a line of guests at the front desk, waiting to check out. One guest, an old pheasant who had been on the stargazing balcony, claimed he had spotted

smoke. "I haven't escaped being hunted all these years to end up being roasted anyway," he said. There was only a wisp of smoke, but it was enough to cause more panic. The line grew even longer.

Mona, Tilly, and Henry served the guests cool drinks, while Mrs. Higgins helped Gilles with checkouts.

"Families first," said a group of five voles, trying to cut in line.

"Families, indeed," said the porcupine in front of them. "That's why *I* must check out first. I must get to my family at once."

"Please!" said Mona. "We live by 'Protect and Respect,' not by—"

One of the voles interrupted, "The hotel can't protect us from fire, now, can it? Where's *your* family? Are they safe?"

He sounded rude, but Mona knew he was just afraid. If she had family, she would want to be with them, too. Could that be why Strawberry wasn't leaving, when all the other guests were?

"The fire is a long way away, sir," Tilly said.

The vole sniffed, and squeezed in behind the porcupine. Mona gave Tilly a grateful glance.

But she noticed Henry still looked scared. "Really, Till? Are you sure?" he whispered. His paw was shaking so much he spilled strawberry iced tea all over the floor.

Tilly didn't get mad, though. "I'm sure," she said. "Everyone's just overreacting. It'll be okay."

It was the most positive Mona had ever seen her friend in the face of a crisis.

When Henry left to get a cloth to clean up, Mona asked, "Do you *really* think we're safe here?" She felt a little like Henry.

"I don't know," said Tilly. "But worrying about it won't put the fire out. Neither will an empty stomach. I can't believe we missed breakfast!"

She reached into her apron pocket and slipped Mona a seedcake. That was Tilly's cure for everything. And sometimes it wasn't such a bad one.

It must have been hard for Tilly to be so positive, because the next day she was grumpier than ever.

Even before breakfast, she and Mona were given a cleaning schedule from Mrs. Higgins and were expected to start right away.

"Who checks out before breakfast?" groaned Tilly, then groaned again when she saw who it was. "The Cavells." She rolled her eyes. "Their room is going to be a mess! It'll need a deep clean for sure. Those bats have been staying here since the fall."

"Bats?" said Mona, surprised. "I don't remember checking in any bats. I don't even remember *seeing* any bats."

"You wouldn't, would you?" said Tilly. "They're bats. They're awake while we're asleep. They would've missed the meeting yesterday—they miss all the important meetings—and must have found out about the fire sometime late last night."

"But . . ." Mona couldn't believe it! She thought she knew all the guests!

"Come on," ordered Tilly. "You better get a bucket and some extra scrubbers. I'll fetch the ladder."

"Ladder?"

Mona knew why when they reached the room. The suite on one of the twig floors was dimly lit and—everything was upside down!

Instead of pegs on the walls and a nest on the floor, like most of the twig suites, in this room, pegs hung from the ceiling. But not just pegs. There were shelves full of books bolted to the ceiling, too. Mona tilted her head but couldn't quite make out the full titles, only the words "Fruit" and "Flying." On the walls were pictures, but they were also upside down for the bats to look at, and even tilting her head didn't help.

Tilly strode to the window to open the shutters.

As the early morning light spilled into the space, Mona could see that it *would* need a thorough clean. There were scuff marks all over the ceiling and fruit stains on the floor. It wasn't too bad, considering— though Tilly didn't seem to think so.

"Long-term guests are supposed to take care of some of their own upkeep," she humphed.

She set up the ladder while Mona started on the floor. It felt good to scrub. Scrubbing was soothing.

Mona was nearly done when she found something behind a fallen book.

"What's this?" she wondered aloud. It was a small blanket made of pounded spiderwebs. She picked it up. It felt so soft, like touching clouds. She could see that there were even tiny green moss stars woven into the webbing. It was beautiful, though it seemed a little worn.

"Great," grumbled Tilly, climbing down from the ladder. "A bat blanket—probably for their pup. They must have forgotten it. We'll have to take it to the Lost and Found."

"There's a Lost and Found?"

"Of course. Didn't you know that?" said Tilly. "Guests leave all sorts of stuff behind. Haven't you noticed? It's like they think we're their personal dustbins!"

"But . . . shouldn't we try to return it?"

"We only return valuable items," replied Tilly. "Not baby blankets."

"But . . ." started Mona again. Though the blanket might not be very expensive, it certainly looked well loved. Didn't that make it valuable?

Mona had felt awful when she lost her walnut suitcase, the one that had belonged to her parents. It had had a heart carved on it, just like the Heartwood's door. Mr. Heartwood had given her a replacement. But it wasn't quite the same.

"Come on, I'll show you where it is. I need a break from that ceiling anyway," said Tilly.

She led the way out of the room to the Lost and Found, which was located in a cupboard beside the upstairs storage room.

"We usually just need one box," said Tilly. "But with everyone leaving in such a rush because of the fire, well, you'll see." She opened the door, and a reed umbrella fell on her, opening with a *POP!*

"Urgh!" Tilly cried.

As Tilly struggled to close the unruly umbrella, Mona stared into the cupboard. It was packed! Boxes were stacked upon boxes, overflowing with items. So many guests, especially families, it seemed, had left things behind. There was a little toy rabbit with one of its ears missing, a teeny-tiny centipede's shoe, a hair bow made of moss, and a book titled *How to Grow Up to Become a Butterfly*.

Tilly tried to put back the umbrella, but when she balanced it on top of a box, the box tipped over, spilling things out across the hallway.

"URGH!" she cried even louder.

As Tilly returned the items to the box, Mona searched for a good place to leave the blanket. What would happen if the bats DID show up again for it and they couldn't find it in the mess? She wanted it to be easy to spot. She wondered if the poor baby bat was missing his blanket right now.

She was about to clear a space for it on a shelf when Tilly said, "Look."

Mona turned to see her holding up something. Something small. "It must have spilled from that box," said Tilly in a hush, all the grumpiness gone from her voice.

Mona stepped closer to take a better look.

In the squirrel's paw was a tiny necklace with a heart-shaped pendant made from a seed. It was identical to the one that Strawberry wore.

"It's got a name carved on it," said Tilly. "Madeline."

"My mom," gasped Mona. "She must have forgotten it here, when she stayed. If my mom had a necklace exactly like Strawberry's . . ."

"Then they *must* be related!" Tilly's tail fluffed up big. "I've never seen a heart-seed necklace before! And TWO of them? I bet they made them together, or maybe they got them when they went on a trip." Tilly's tail fluffed up even bigger and knocked over another box. She didn't seem to care.

"Mona, Strawberry's your aunt. She's got to be. She's the one. . . ."

That reminded Mona of Strawberry's letter. "That's just what SHE said, in a letter . . . about me . . . I think. . . ."

"Think? There's no thinking about it. You should've told me right away! Mona, that's *proof*!"

"But why hasn't she said anything?"

Tilly rolled her eyes. "Don't you know *anything* about secrets yet?"

Mona thought she did. But maybe she didn't. There was one thing she knew, though. "Tilly, without this we would have never found the necklace," she said, holding up the baby blanket. "Please, can't we send it back to the bats?"

"Oh, Mona! Only *you* would think of *bats* at a time like this."

But she said it with a grin, which meant yes.

Stories and Snacks

"I have family," Mona kept whispering to herself throughout the day, reaching into her apron pocket to touch the necklace. There was nothing she wanted more.

Except perhaps for Tilly to stop pestering her. "Has she said anything yet?" asked Tilly, for what felt like the millionth time.

"No," replied Mona. "But she will. Don't you know anything about secrets?" she teased.

Tilly groaned. "Seriously, if everyone just said what they knew when they knew it, everything would be a whole lot easier!"

That might be the case, Mona thought, *but it hardly ever happens.* She'd been thinking a lot about why Strawberry hadn't told her yet. Maybe Strawberry was just waiting for the perfect time to share her secret. Happy secrets *were* best told at happy times, Mona decided.

Now was definitely not one of those times. Everyone was too upset about the fire—and rightly so. Although it was still far away, and hadn't moved beyond the Foothills, it was impossible to predict what would happen. A heavy rain could put it out, but a strong wind could make it spread.

"Pebbly Patch is between the fire and here," Mr. Heartwood kept reassuring everyone. "The rocks won't let the flames come near."

Once Tilly explained the patch was actually very big, and fire couldn't burn on rocks, Mona felt better.

But Mr. Heartwood's words didn't soothe the

guests. The next day, there was no checkout schedule posted. All the guests had gone. And there were
no check-in duties either. Everyone had cancelled.
Mrs. Higgins gave Mona and Tilly a list of tasks
instead, things no one usually had time for:

- ♡ -

1. Manage mysterious mushrooms on the trunk floors.

2. Source the skunky smell in the honeymoon suite.

3. Clean the hive room.

"Be ready to get sticky," grumped Tilly.
"Captain Ruby and her squadron left in a hurry. I
guess bees and smoke don't mix. What a summer!
You're lucky we got that blanket out. Mail service
suspended! Half the staff gone home! More work

for us . . . and not even the Summer Picnic to look forward to."

Summer Picnic? Mona hadn't known they were planning one.

"What's the Picnic?" she asked.

"It was a new summer festival Mrs. Higgins was planning. Mostly it was going to be eating. That's what you do at a picnic, eat and tell stories."

It sounded like a happy time, the kind Mona was hoping for.

"Why can't we have a picnic anyway?" she suggested. "A small one for the staff. There's lots of food, isn't there, with no guests?"

Tilly's eyes glinted. "Bet your beechnuts. Mona, that's a great idea!"

Mr. Heartwood thought so, too. "A bit of fun would help everyone," he agreed. So Mona and Tilly got to work, finishing their tasks in a flurry. Tilly seemed especially determined. Food did that to her. Mona didn't think you could scrub a hive with your tail, but Tilly proved her wrong. Mind you, it took Tilly twice as long to wash up afterward. But she didn't grump once.

As soon as they were clean, Mona helped Strawberry prepare a picnic basket, with dandelion sorbet and iced nettle tea and sandwiches made with acorn bread. Tilly and Henry, meanwhile, gathered blankets. Alone in the kitchen with Strawberry, Mona was tempted to ask her about the necklaces. But Strawberry's attention was focused on the food—and the fire.

"I know Pebbly Patch," she said, scooping the sorbet. "I picnicked there once a long time ago. It *is* big, but . . ." She paused. "You think the wild is going to behave one way . . . but it's not like a kitchen. You can't ever predict it."

Mona saw Strawberry's paws were trembling. "Don't worry. I'm sure Mr. Heartwood will keep us safe."

Strawberry gave a shaky laugh. "Of course, of course, sugar. Everything will be fine."

Or maybe it wouldn't.

As soon as everyone gathered outside, ready to set up, Henry started complaining.

"It smells really bad out here," he said. "You know how sensitive my nose is." He held his tail over his face.

Henry was right. Outside, the air was starting to smell of smoke. And even though it was only early evening, it was already dark. A haze covered the sky like a shutter. Was the fire spreading?

Before Mona could ask Mr. Heartwood, Henry continued, his voice muffled through his fur, "Mrflmrflmrfl *Onions.*"

"Did you say 'Onions'?" asked Mona.

Henry nodded and removed his tail, crinkling his nose instead. "Yes, the Night of *Too* Many Onions," he replied. "This kind of reminds me of it." Henry rubbed his nose.

 67

"If only onions were the cause." Mr. Heartwood grimaced at the smoky sky. "Time for us to move our paws."

So much for the picnic.

Disappointed, Mona followed Mr. Heartwood as he led the staff to the lobby. He plopped the picnic basket down on the rug and made a surprise announcement: "With no guests here, we have no guests to lose. . . . We can have our picnic wherever we choose."

A picnic in the lobby!

They pushed back all the furniture, and Mona and Tilly laid out the blankets on the rug. Mrs. Higgins brought up extra-soft pillows to sit on, usually reserved for guests. "Try not to drip on them," she said, looking right at Henry.

Henry didn't seem to be listening.

"These pillows are the best—and the bounciest," he said, helping himself to a sandwich from the picnic basket. He peered suspiciously between

the slices of acorn bread. "There aren't . . ."

Mona shook her head no.

"Good," he said, taking a big bite. Through a mouthful of food, he began, "At the orpflmrfl . . ."

"Chew before chatting," reminded Tilly.

Henry gulped. "At the orphanage, Hood once stole a bag of potatoes that turned out to be onions.

 69

We had to eat onion soup and onion stew and onion sandwiches. We covered our faces, but soon we were all crying anyway. Hood said, 'You can't hate onions that much!' But it was just the onions making us cry. They actually tasted pretty good. But I got sick of them."

"I could never get sick of anything," said Tilly, reaching into the picnic basket. Mona giggled.

A quiet lull fell over everyone as they helped themselves to food. Mona nibbled a cheese sandwich that Strawberry had made specially for her. It was strange sitting on the floor, but fun, too. A chance to finally relax.

Zzzzzzzzzzzz . . .

It seemed some could relax more than others!

"Oh, Henry," said Tilly. She tried to wake him up but couldn't.

"At least he *can* sleep," said Mrs. Higgins.

"Shhh!" said Mr. Higgins. "Don't tell *that* story." He gave Mrs. Higgins a concerned look.

"Ah, the Tunnel of Two Hearts," said Gilles, ignoring Mr. Higgins and settling back into his pillow, resting his claws on his belly. "Dug to save a marriage."

"What do you mean?" asked Mona.

"When Mr. and Mrs. Higgins first got married," said Gilles, "Mr. Higgins had insomnia and couldn't sleep. And that meant Mrs. Higgins couldn't sleep either. And you know how early SHE has to get up. So, she did what she does best. She put Mr. Higgins to work. Not cleaning, or cooking, or decluttering. But digging. Outside, where he wouldn't disturb any of the guests."

"I figured he might dig a hole big enough to use as an extra cellar," said Mrs. Higgins. "But the tunnel goes all the way from the garden to the stream, now, doesn't it, dear?"

Mr. Higgins shrugged.

"A secret tunnel?" said Mona, nearly choking on the last bite of her sandwich.

"Let's keep it that way," said Tilly, looking at her sleeping brother. "Or we'll never see Henry again."

"Don't worry, it's boarded up now." Mr. Higgins sighed. "If only I had tried chamomile tea earlier. Right, Mr. Heartwood?"

Mr. Heartwood nodded, but he wasn't looking at Mr. Higgins. His eyes were fixed on the sign, "PROTECT AND RESPECT," that hung above the fireplace. "Did I ever tell you the story of our sign?"

Everyone shook their heads.

"I always thought it was because . . ." said Mona, "because . . ." She couldn't bring herself to say it.

"Because one guest tried to eat another guest," Tilly finished for her.

Mr. Heartwood smiled. "No, not at all. Though eating *was* involved. And sleeping, too, might I add. But no snoring or digging."

Another story? Mona pricked up her ears. She was liking picnics more and more.

72

Tilly passed her a cup of the dandelion sorbet, while Mr. Heartwood leaned back into his twig chair. It creaked under his weight. "It was long ago, when the hotel had just opened and we had our very first guests," he began. "One morning I awoke to find pieces of the tree were disappearing from the inside. Surely it couldn't be. Who would eat our tree?" He paused before continuing, "The next morning, it was the same. Some guests even thought the Heartwood might have a ghost."

"A ghost!" burst out Mona and Tilly, exchanging a wide-eyed glance.

Mr. Heartwood chuckled and continued, "Then one morning, I woke earlier than usual, to find a beaver chewing on the mantel."

"NO!" cried Gilles, horrified.

"Indeed!" said Mr. Heartwood. "I was furious. How dare he eat part of my hotel! I asked him to go, I didn't know . . ."

"Didn't know what?" piped up Mona.

 73

"Didn't know that the beaver was a sleepwalker—*and* a sleep-eater. The poor chap had no clue what he was doing, and was dismayed at the damage. He sent me a gift—that sign you see there—to show that he cared. His name was Benjamin."

"Benjamin, your friend?" asked Mona.

"Yes." Mr. Heartwood nodded. "That was the start of a friendship that has continued to this day."

The stories continued, too. There were *so* many about the Heartwood. Some Mona knew, but most she hadn't heard. It made her proud, all the extraordinary things that had happened at the hotel.

Soon, the sorbet cups had been licked clean, so Strawberry fetched more snacks and iced tea. Mona snuggled deep into her pillow, stories swirling around her like rose petals in the wind.

Only one story was missing, the one Mona most wanted to hear. She knew this was the happy moment she had been waiting for. So when there was a pause in the storytelling, Mona piped up, "What about you, Strawberry? Do you have a story?"

"Yes!" said Tilly, catching on right away.

Strawberry took a deep breath. "I do."

"Is it about your hotel? The Inn Between?" asked Gilles eagerly.

"In a way," said Strawberry. "But really it's about . . ." She looked right at Mona.

Mona felt a happy shiver go up and down her tail. This was it. At last, Strawberry was going to share her secret, and everyone would know that she was Mona's aunt.

Before Strawberry could begin, there was a *SCRITCH-SCRATCH* on the door, followed by a loud *YIP!*

Strawberry jumped. They all did.

"It's a wolf!" exclaimed Mrs. Higgins, clutching Mr. Higgins's paw. "They've found us at last!"

THE GROWLING GUEST

The time for Strawberry's story had passed—for now.

"Hurry!" said Mr. Heartwood, leading the way downstairs. Tilly and Henry raced after him, followed by Mr. and Mrs. Higgins, Gilles, and Strawberry. "If the wolf finds the latch on the door, he'll get inside. We have to hide!"

Mr. Heartwood was right. Mona remembered how Brumble had almost opened the door. Everyone had been scared then, too.

But . . . Mona paused. The bear had only been

there because he'd mistaken the Heartwood for his winter den. He'd just needed directions.

Mona listened again, more carefully.

YIP! YIP!

It didn't sound like a wolf. Mona knew what wolves sounded like. She'd been right beside them in the fall, when they'd tried to attack the Heartwood. And this animal didn't sound hungry or fierce, either. It sounded scared.

I can find out what's really going on, thought Mona. *I can use the back door and go around the tree. I'm small. Whatever it is won't see me.*

So instead of catching up with the others, she took a few steps past the staircase.

"Where are you going, sugar?" came Strawberry's voice.

Mona turned to see the mouse, looking up at her from the stairs. Her tail was trembling.

"Mona, you must come with us at once!"

 77

"But . . ." stammered Mona. "It sounds like it's crying. I think it's hurt."

"It's a wolf!" said Strawberry.

"No, it's not," said Mona. "It's . . ."

YIP!

Before Mona could explain, the noise came again. Strawberry stepped up, reached out and grabbed Mona's paw. "I can't let you go!"

Mona knew her aunt was already worried about the fire. Was she afraid of everything outside the hotel? "I'll be fine," Mona said, and tried to pull her paw away.

Strawberry's grip, however, tightened. When her aunt began down the stairs, Mona had no choice but to follow. By the time they were halfway down, Strawberry relaxed her hold, and Mona slipped her paw away.

Although they were muffled now, she could still hear the yips. And Strawberry must have, too, because her fur bristled and she scurried down-stairs even faster.

Her aunt was clearly very scared. *But I'm not*, Mona thought, a little surprised. She was actually more curious and worried. When the yips grew more frequent, Mona knew she had to investigate. She couldn't stand to think of another animal in pain.

Strawberry was out of sight now, and didn't seem to realize Mona had stopped following. This was Mona's chance. She hurried quietly up the stairs, along the hallway to the back door, and pushed it open.

Outside, day was breaking. They had been telling stories all night long!

Carefully, she tiptoed past the garden, around the tree, toward the front door.

There it was! Even in the hazy pink light, Mona could see it *wasn't* a wolf. It was a fox!

The fox was right at the door, but he was lying

on his side, his tail spread out behind him like a trail of embers. He was small, a spring-born pup, and he seemed very still, until . . . *YIP!* He called out again, and scratched at the door.

Mona squeaked in fear.

The fox lifted his head and turned to look at her. His teeth were bared, sharp as thorns.

Every muscle in Mona froze. She should have gone with Strawberry! What was she thinking?

But when the fox tried to stand, he yelped and lay back down. He started licking at one paw, and Mona noticed it was swollen.

He wasn't there to hurt anyone. He was hurt himself.

"Wh-what happened?" Mona stammered.

But the fox only raised his head and gazed at her with his big amber eyes. Could he even speak? Maybe he was just learning.

Mona tried again. "Where's your family?" she asked.

The fox tensed, then looked at his paw.

"Did something happen to them? Was it the fire?"

The fox's ears twitched.

Mona gulped. Did that mean yes?

"It's okay, the fire isn't here," she said gently. "You're okay."

She wasn't sure, though. How would he manage? Mona had been young like him when her parents died, and that had been hard enough. She couldn't imagine what it would have been like if she'd been injured, too.

Mona knew she shouldn't—even small and hurt, he was *still* a fox—but she couldn't help herself.

"Wait," she said. "I'll be right back."

As quickly as her paws could take her, Mona rushed inside, through the back door. She was too afraid to go around the fox and use the front one. In the lobby, she found what she wanted. She took a case off one of the puffy pillows and grabbed a half-filled jug of iced tea. She knew she shouldn't take things without asking, but it was the right thing to do.

The fox was still at the front door. His eyes were closed now. Was he . . . ?

Mona squeaked, unsure of what to do, and the fox's eyes opened.

"Yip, yip, yip," he whined.

"I'm here," said Mona. "Shush . . ." Slowly, hesitantly, she approached the fox.

"Shush," she said again. "Just stay still." Carefully she tipped some tea on to his sore paw, to wash

 82

and cool it. The fox whimpered but didn't move. Then, her own paws shaking, she wrapped the pillowcase around the fox's, folding the cloth over to make sure his claws didn't poke through. She could barely breathe while she tied the bow.

"There, done," she said, letting out her breath. "That will feel much better. Trust me, I've hurt my paw before, too."

The fox's tail thumped on the ground as if in thanks, and a small smile lifted the corners of his mouth. Suddenly—the smile turned to a snarl!

Mona jumped back in alarm. Had he tricked her?

"Enough, young stranger; I'm no danger," came a familiar voice.

Mona turned. The fox wasn't snarling at her. He was snarling at Mr. Heartwood. The badger stood there, taller and sterner than ever. His arms were crossed. "Miss Mouse, please go inside," he ordered. "Strawberry said you were here, but I reassured her you knew better. Clearly not."

"But Mr. Heartwood, he's hurt. . . . He's just a pup. I don't think he knows how to talk yet."

"Yes, I see that, Miss Mouse." He uncrossed his arms and pointed back to the hotel. "Below you must go!"

Mona knew when she had to obey the big badger, and now was one of those times.

As she was leaving, she gave a backward glance at the fox. "My name's Mona," she said, not expecting a reply.

To her surprise, the fox whispered, "Blaze."

Down in the kitchen, Strawberry, Tilly, and Henry were relieved to see her, though Strawberry was still shaken. "I thought you were behind me," she said, but was interrupted by Henry, who clamored, "What happened?"

Mona tried to say, but no words came out. The story was so new it wasn't ready for telling. It was too sad. Too strange. She wasn't supposed to care for a fox. Foxes . . . they didn't live by "Protect and Respect." The fire had made everything all mixed-up.

"Give Mona a chance to catch her breath," said Tilly, passing her friend a glass of cool water. "You're okay, right?"

Mona nodded. She drank the water slowly, savoring each sip, much to Henry's frustration.

When she was finally finished, he burst out, "You've caught your breath, now, haven't you, Mona? Tell us . . ."

But before she had a chance, Mr. Heartwood strode into the room.

"Is Blaze all right?" Mona asked.

"Blaze? Who's Blaze?" said Henry.

Mr. Heartwood took off his hat and set it aside. "The fox—" started Mr. Heartwood.

"Fox?!" cried Henry, his eyes wide.

Strawberry gasped.

 85

"Yes. The fox. He is much better," said Mr. Heartwood, answering Mona's question. "In fact, he has left. And now you must, too."

He made a sweeping gesture that included all of them, then sank into his chair, looking suddenly smaller than Mona had ever seen him.

"Mr. Heartwood, you don't mean . . ." started Mona.

"Yes, I do," said the badger, tugging at his whiskers. "It is time to leave the Heartwood Hotel."

A Friends' Farewell

Mr. Heartwood's voice grew louder and louder in Mona's ears as he continued speaking. "Although we don't know what it will do, one thing is true. The fire might not reach here, but more wolves and coyotes will. The flames are pushing them out of their homes. This fox was young and hurt. He wasn't a danger to us. But we don't know what others might be like. I cannot take that risk. You must leave today. Right away."

Leave the Heartwood? The Heartwood was her home! Mona had spent years wandering from one home to another. She couldn't do it again. "What about Mrs. Prickles? When she gets back from her honeymoon, she won't know where we've all gone."

"She won't be venturing *into* the forest. No one will. Not right now," assured Mr. Heartwood. "It's not safe."

"The fire hasn't crossed Pebbly Patch, has it?" asked Strawberry, her voice quavering slightly. "If it does . . ."

"It won't," said Mr. Heartwood.

He must have seen Mona's worried look, however, because he sat up straighter and continued, firmly, "Please, dear friends, this is merely a safety measure, and temporary. Once the fire is over, we will return."

Everybody relaxed, including Mona, but she noticed his words didn't rhyme.

"Mr. Heartwood is right," said Mr. Higgins. "Come on, Henrietta. It's time to stay with our children."

Mona didn't know Mr. and Mrs. Higgins had children!

"I was thinking of staying at the Beaver Lodge," said Gilles.

"Yes, yes," said Mr. Heartwood, though he looked distracted.

"But," continued the lizard, "perhaps I'll pay my parents a visit instead."

Gilles had a mom and dad? Of course he did. Yet it still seemed strange to Mona. *Where will I go?* she wondered. *Where's Tilly going?*

Henry had the answer. "We'll go to Hood and Hazeline's, right, Till?"

"Right," answered Tilly. "It's much farther from the fire. We'll be safe there."

Before Mona could ask if she was going with them, Strawberry turned to her. "I hope you'll come with me to the Inn Between."

Mona was so surprised, she didn't know what to say.

But Tilly did. "Of course she will."

Strawberry smiled. "Are you sure, sugar?" she asked Mona.

Mona wasn't sure of anything right now. Still, she nodded. "Thank you," she said.

Mona was quiet, but Tilly couldn't stop talking on the way back to Mona's room.

"I'm so glad you said yes," said Tilly.

"But . . ." started Mona. "I didn't . . ."

"You do want to be with family, don't you?" Tilly interrupted. "Strawberry is family, Mona. *Real* family." Her voice wobbled. "And you might find even more family at the Inn Between."

Mona hadn't thought of that. "But . . . I thought *we . . .*"

"This is for the best," said Tilly, sounding matter-of-fact now. "You don't belong at Hood's. Hood's is for orphans. You're not an orphan anymore."

 90

That wasn't exactly true, but Tilly continued, "You'll have so much fun with Strawberry. I know you will. You'd better not let any of those mice boss you around, though. You're only there for a visit. You work *here*, after all. And *I* trained you. You'd better tell them that."

"I will," said Mona. "I promise. But, Till . . ."

"Yeah, yeah." Tilly sniffed and blinked hard. "You can thank me later."

When Tilly left, Mona began to pack, her head swirling with thoughts of the fire and everything Tilly had said. She took out her walnut suitcase with the heart-shaped clasps, the one Mr. Heartwood had given her. Mr. Heartwood had said that it wasn't a case with which to roam, but a place to store her things, now that the Heartwood was her home.

What had Tilly told her? She wasn't going to be gone for long. She put the suitcase back. All she needed was her apron, and the seed necklace, which she slipped in the apron's pocket, the one with the heart Tilly had sewn on it. It was lopsided, but perfect.

Tilly's right, thought Mona. Everyone else was going with their families. And now she was, too. *Just for a visit.*

She felt a quiver of excitement in her stomach, like a cluster of tiny butterflies. She was going to be spending time with her aunt. She was going to the Inn Between! Soon she'd return with her own story to tell Tilly and everyone else, in the grand Heartwood lobby.

But when Mona left her room, the door closed with a final click, like it was saying good-bye.

The Frightening Forest

Outside the Heartwood, the air didn't just smell smoky—you could taste it. Blaze was gone, as Mr. Heartwood had said. Strawberry and Tilly, though, kept glancing cautiously, this way and that.

In the spring, the staff had gathered to see Mr. Heartwood off when he'd gone away to help his friend build the grand Beaver Lodge. This time it was the opposite. Mr. Heartwood stood at the door of his hotel while the last of the staff left.

Instead of his tie and top hat, he was wearing an old vest that had patches, and a pair of work gloves.

"But Mr. Heartwood, what about you?" asked
Mona.

"I'll be fine," he said. "I just have a few things
to finish."

"Then you must go to the Beaver Lodge, Mr.
Heartwood," said Mrs. Higgins sternly.

"Yes, yes, of course," said Mr. Heartwood.

Mrs. Higgins gave him a doubtful look. "You
promise, Georgie?"

 94

Tilly nudged Mona. "Georgie?"

Mona would've laughed, except Mrs. Higgins looked so serious.

Mr. Heartwood didn't say more. Instead he took a step back into the hotel.

"Be swift, stay safe." Mr. Heartwood waved and went inside.

But no one moved to leave, until at last, Henry tugged Tilly's paw. "I want to see Hood! Let's go!"

And so they did. Everyone headed up the dry streambed—there was no sign of water now, not even a trickle. Only Mona and Strawberry went a different way. Strawberry pointed to a path between some bushes, where wild strawberry plants were growing.

"To the village—and the Inn Between," she said, smiling at Mona. She had been smiling at her ever since Mona had agreed to come with her. "Follow me," she said.

Mona was about to when she heard Tilly cry,

"Mona, wait!" Tilly ran up to her with a seedcake in her paw. She split it in half and held one piece out to Mona. "Here," she said.

"It's okay," said Mona. "I'm not hungry."

"It isn't for eating," said Tilly. "It's for keeping. You know: 'Break to Bye, and Have at Hi.' It's a squirrel thing. Just . . . just don't eat it, okay?"

Tilly pressed the seedcake into Mona's paw. Mona stared down at it. It was small and ragged and looked a bit like half a heart. "Oh, Tilly . . ."

But her best friend was already gone.

Mona carefully wrapped the piece of seed-cake in a leaf and slipped it into her apron pocket, then hurried after Strawberry. "Stay close," said Strawberry, sounding serious.

The bow on Strawberry's hat bobbed as they made their way along the path. The wedding rain-storm was long forgotten. Everything was dusty and brown. The dry moss crackled under Mona's paws.

They weren't the only ones leaving Fernwood. Along the way, they saw a warren of rabbits, including aunts, uncles, nieces, nephews, and a frantic great-great grandmother trying to keep count. A trio of deer, bounding briskly through the trees, but still as graceful as dancers. A family of chipmunks, scrambling out of a burrow, with suitcase after suitcase. "Too much! Too much!" the father chipmunk was saying. "But the tea towels!" the mother chipmunk cried back.

Mona didn't hear the end of their conversation, because Strawberry urged her on. "There's still a long way to go. I can't wait for you to see the Inn Between, sugar. Everything there is the right size for us."

"I guess it makes cleaning easier," said Mona matter-of-factly.

Strawberry smiled. "It certainly does. Though I don't mind cleaning."

"There *is* something nice about straightening a room . . ." said Mona.

"And sweeping a floor . . ." continued Strawberry.

"And putting everything just so," finished Mona.

Now she smiled. More things they had in common. This might not be the perfect time, but it was good enough. "Strawberry, I wanted to—"

"It will have to wait," interrupted Strawberry. "We aren't going to be able to sleep in a neat, clean room tonight unless we hurry." She picked up the pace, almost leaving Mona behind.

Mona let out a groan that would have made Tilly proud. She'd missed her chance *again*.

She hurried to catch up with Strawberry, but lost

sight of her at a fork in the path. She started down the way that looked more traveled. Strawberry's voice stopped her.

"No, Mona, not that way!" There was panic in her voice. "We can't take that path. It might get us there in half the time, but it's more likely we'll get eaten. It's not worth the risk. That's where . . ." She shivered and couldn't seem to finish.

She didn't have to. Mona saw the tracks of large animals. Her fur bristled, and she scurried after Strawberry down the other trail, which was tiny and hidden.

They traveled for a long time together, only stopping to drink. Eventually the air smelled less smoky, perhaps because there was now a breeze. Mona felt it on her fur, like hot breath. The sky was still dark—though maybe that was only because it was growing late. Mona *was* getting tired. Her paws hurt and her stomach grumbled. But Strawberry didn't stop for a snack.

The farther they were from the Heartwood, the stranger the forest grew. Mona could hear the sounds of other animals on the move. Was that the snuffling of porcupines? The scrabbling of voles?

Mona stuck even closer to Strawberry, almost tripping on her tail.

AWOOOO! There was a howl. It didn't sound like a fox this time. It sounded like a wolf! Mr. Heartwood *had* said that the fire would drive all animals from their homes, even those who lived by "Tooth and Claw." If the safe path was this scary, what would the other path have been like?

"Faster," Strawberry urged, breaking into a run. Mona did, too, and tripped over Strawberry's tail, sending them both tumbling off the path and into a thicket.

Strawberry found her suitcase and pulled Mona up, then looked around frantically. The thicket was a maze of branches and roots. Mona tried to stay calm. She spied an opening between two twisted twigs.

"Come on," she said, tugging on Strawberry's paw. She led her aunt through the tangle of branches. "Are you sure this is the way?" Strawberry asked.

Mona wasn't, but she kept going.

When they emerged, there was no sign of the path. "We're lost!" cried Strawberry. Panic rose in Mona, too. Where was the path?

The thicket stretched into the darkness. Mona couldn't see its end. But she *could* see something. A strangely familiar sight, a small blanket, one end caught on a branch, another in the claws of a little bat. A mother and father bat hovered above.

"Wait, Mama! I CAN'T sleep without it," said the little bat.

"Yes, yes, don't I know it! But hurry up. Uncle Cavell is expecting us."

"The Cavells!" piped up Mona.

"Hello?" said the mother bat. She must have heard Mona. "Who's there?"

"Down here!" said Mona. "Could you help us?"

The mother bat swooped down, while the father and baby kept working to free his blanket. "A mouse?" She peered at Mona closely, her eyes resting on the apron. "Are you from the Heartwood?"

Mona nodded. "Though we're trying to get to the village. It's safer, but we lost the path."

"The path? It's just over there, around that corner of the thicket." She pointed one wing.

"Oh, thank you!" said Strawberry, finding her voice.

"Oh, no, thank *you*. It was so nice of the Heartwood staff to send us our blanket. Bartholomew really can't sleep without it. And things are tough enough right now without losing sleep."

Mona smiled.

"MAMA! I got it!" the little bat cried triumphantly.

"Great job, Barty!" The mother bat turned her gaze back to Mona. "We really must be going."

"Us too," said Mona. "Thank you again."

The bats disappeared up into the darkness, in a series of flits and flaps, the blanket in Barty's claws blowing behind him in the breeze.

The path was exactly where Mrs. Cavell had said.

Mona's fear had vanished. If only Tilly was with her. She'd see that it'd been worth it to return the blanket. *I'll tell her when I see her again*, Mona thought. But when would that be? She felt a small ache begin in her chest.

She was reaching into her pocket to feel for the piece of seedcake Tilly had given her, when Strawberry cried, "Look!"

Mona's heart leapt up.

They had come to the end of the forest. There, carved on a sign, just Mona's height, was an arrow with the words:

The Inn Between

Other signs on the post read, CRUMBCAKE BAKERY, WHISKERTOP TOURS, and THE BED AND BREADCRUMB.

"Our competition," confided Strawberry.

The final sign pointed back toward the path they hadn't taken. DANGER, it read.

"Don't worry about that," said Strawberry. She seemed much more confident now that they were out of the forest. "There's no danger at the Inn Between. Not even cats. Once we cross here, we're perfectly safe."

In front of them stretched a giant path, like a river made of stone. Instead of the stars, enormous

lamps along the side of it lit their way as they scurried across.

Once they were on the other side, they stopped for a moment in a patch of grass to catch their breath. The breeze had turned into a bluster, and the blades of grass swished back and forth like angry tails.

Holding her hat on with one paw and her suitcase in the other, Strawberry pushed through the grasses. Mona did, too.

There in front of them rose a giant house, with a door many, many times bigger than the Heartwood's. Even in the lamplight, Mona could see that it was painted bright blue, with fancy green frills hanging from its windows, like moss. Its chimney stuck up like a crooked treetop.

Another sign hung across the house's door. THE INN, it read.

"*This* is it?" squeaked Mona.

"Yes," said Strawberry. "I mean, no. You'll see. Follow me."

Mona felt a strange mix of nervousness and excitement as Strawberry led them around the side of the house, through patches of berry plants. "That's how I got my name," said Strawberry. "All my family is named after different berries."

So my mom should be, too. But Madeline isn't a berry name, thought Mona.

She didn't have a chance to think on that further, because Strawberry stopped at a large drainpipe coming down from the roof. Mona wasn't sure why until she saw another sign, PLEASE RING FOR SERVICE, and a bell, hanging from the opening.

"No need to wake them," said Strawberry. "Up we go."

Strawberry went first. Inside, the drain was surprisingly clean, and brightly lit with a string of teeny-tiny lights that glowed without fire. Steps, like the rungs of a ladder, led up the steepest parts.

Halfway up, Strawberry stopped in front of a small door cut into the side of the drain. A big black button served as a doorknob.

Mona's heart pounded. A new hotel. With the fire, and Tilly, there hadn't been a chance to get properly excited. But it *was* exciting. She was going to see another hotel—a *mouse* hotel! More than that—in this hotel, in the cozy quiet, she knew the

time would be right at last. Finally, she would hear Strawberry's story.

Strawberry held the knob and pushed. The door squeaked open, and together they climbed across a flat wooden bridge, with little dark notches on one side, through another door . . . and into the Inn Between.

The lobby was just as tidy as the Heartwood's but much smaller, and how different!

The furniture, instead of being made of twigs and moss, bark and berries, was made of things she'd only heard about. Buttons and bottle caps were balanced on thimbles for tables, and there were spools of thread for chairs. Another chair was made of the top of a wooden spoon—but an enormous one. There was no fireplace, but heat seemed to be rising from a cluster of pinprick-size holes in the floor.

One thing, however, reminded her of the Heartwood. Hanging from the wall, sewn onto a large ribbon, was a motto: HAPPINESS LIES IN BETWEEN.

Just like Strawberry had said, everything was the right size for a mouse. It even smelled mousy. Mona couldn't wait to see the rest of the hotel.

To one side of the lobby, a giant upside-down teacup served as a desk. Behind it sat an old mouse—asleep. Gilles would be shocked! There was another little bell, like the one at the entrance, positioned in front of her, and a sign that read RING TO WAKE.

But they didn't need to.

Suddenly, the old mouse jerked upright. Mona jumped.

"Hruup!" the old mouse snorted. Her fur was a dull gray, but her eyes shone bright as she gazed first at Strawberry and then at Mona.

"Took you long enough! Have you any idea how worried I was?"

"Grandma Gooseberry, what are you doing waiting up for us?" stammered Strawberry.

"Grandma?" whispered Mona. More family already?

"I didn't expect—" continued Strawberry.

"Expect? What else would you expect, after the news I've heard? My granddaughter, staying in the very path of danger!"

"But, Grandma, we weren't. Why, the fire wasn't even a threat to us. Actually, it was a fox who posed the most—"

"Hruup!" snorted Grandma Gooseberry again. "Wrong, wrong!"

"What do you mean, wrong?" piped up Mona. Her heart was beating faster now—for a different reason.

The old mouse pointed her whiskers at Mona, then asked Strawberry, "Is this her?"

Strawberry nodded.

Grandma Gooseberry pulled a pair of glasses from her apron pocket and put them on. They made her eyes twice as large. She peered at Mona. Mona stood up straighter.

"Well, well. Small thing, aren't you? Just like your mother at that age. . . ." Her voice caught and she took off her glasses and dabbed at her eyes with a bit of lace. "Well, I'm certainly glad you brought her, Strawberry. Didn't know if you had it in you to brave the forest twice. Thought I might have to come and get you myself. I suppose she'll be living with us now."

"What? No! I . . ." stammered Mona.

"Oh, you are quite welcome here. Don't mind me. I'm nicer than I seem, as Strawberry will tell . . ."

"Tell me what's happened!" cried Mona.

"Grandma Gooseberry, we don't understand," said Strawberry.

"You didn't hear it from the hummingbird? You didn't feel the wind?" Grandma Gooseberry clutched her bit of lace. "That hummingbird said the news was bad, and indeed it was. Very bad. The worst."

Grandma Gooseberry took a deep breath—and Mona did, too.

"The wind has shifted the fire. It's passed Pebbly Patch. It's headed for the Heartwood."

Strawberry's Secret

Instantly, Mona felt faint. Everything turned hazy, like smoke had filled her head.

The lobby swirled around her as Grandma Gooseberry went on. "I know you did what you could. I heard about the trench and the buckets of water. But it's a good thing you left them as you did."

What trench? What buckets of water? Maybe she wasn't hearing clearly. Grandma Gooseberry's voice sounded like it was coming from far away. "It's only a matter of time before flames find the tree, or so the hummingbird said. *Tsk-tsk.*"

 115

Mona closed her eyes to stop the swirling. This wasn't supposed to happen! Mr. Heartwood said the fire wouldn't reach the hotel.

"Mona!" came a voice. Strawberry's.

"She needs a cup of tea and crumbs, that's what. When did you last feed her, Strawberry?"

"She just needs to rest. Here, sugar, come," Strawberry said. Mona felt Strawberry take her paw.

There was a loud noise like the ringing of a bell, and then more voices. Mona saw and heard everything like she was in a dream. Strawberry, leading her down a hall to a room and a bed, with a quilt made of ribbons. A ladybug in the tiniest polka-dotted apron, carrying a tray with a crumb on it. And a cricket with a thimble of water, or was it tea?

It *was* tea, iced tea, sweet and cool. And the crumb buttery and crisp. Slowly, the haze cleared.

Mona realized she was propped up on a bed in a small guest room.

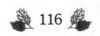

116

Beside the bed was a nightstand, covered with another ribbon for a tablecloth. In a corner, a giant pencil stood upright, a bathrobe hanging from it. On the wall was a picture of a graceful mouse.

"That's the prima ballerina for the Mouseco Ballet," chirped the cricket. "She stayed in this very room! Many famous mice have used it to retreat and recover from the hurry-scurry of the outside world. And now you. You are famous here

yourself, you know. Why, we've never even had a *Pinecone* review yet. But the Heartwood Hotel has been featured in the paper *three* times! And from what we hear it was all thanks to you."

"Hush, James," said Strawberry. "This is not the time. Thank you for the tea. You can leave now."

"Yes, of course," said the cricket, scuttling out, leaving Strawberry and Mona alone.

"James is very proud of the Inn Between," said Strawberry, straightening the quilt. "There. Are you feeling better?"

Maybe a little, thought Mona, *but not really*. How could she be?

"It's going to be okay," Strawberry said. "You're here, and you're safe. Bless the berries Mr. Heartwood made us all leave when he did."

"The Heartwood . . . it's my home." Mona gulped.

"I know," said Strawberry. "But you don't have

to worry. The Inn Between can be your home now." She gestured around the room. "It's as much yours as mine. There . . . there's something I need to tell you. Something I've been meaning to tell you for a while now."

Now? *Now* was when Strawberry was going to tell her the happy secret? This was the worst time of all!

"I know," blurted Mona, before Strawberry had a chance. Mona sat up and pulled out the necklace from her apron pocket.

Strawberry's eyes went wide. "How . . . ? Where—where did you get this?"

"Tilly and I found it in the Lost and Found," said Mona.

She passed the necklace to Strawberry, who held it carefully, almost tenderly. Her voice trembled as she said, "Your mom and I made these for each other when we were very young."

"Tilly and me, we figured it out," said Mona.

 119

"I was hoping you would," said Strawberry.

"It was mostly Tilly."

Strawberry nodded. "She's a smart squirrel. Best friends must have a nose for each other."

Mona wasn't sure what that meant—but she knew Tilly would like the "smart" part. She couldn't wait to tell her, to tell her everything. Except, if the Heartwood was gone, if she was living here, when would she see her friend again? Mona must have let out a sob, because Strawberry pulled her close.

"There, there," said Strawberry. "Chin up, buttercup. Everything's going to be fine. Now you know why my home, my hotel, is yours."

"Why didn't you tell me right away?" asked Mona.

"Because," said Strawberry, slowly, "once I told you some of my story, you would want to know all, and then . . ." Her voice faltered. "Then I was afraid you might not want anything to do with me. I hoped if you got to know me a bit first that might help."

"What do you mean?"

Strawberry shook her head. "I . . . I don't think it's a story I should tell you right now, either. It should wait."

"No, *tell* me," Mona insisted. Happy time or not, she needed to hear it.

"Very well," said Strawberry. A quiver had crept into her voice. "It was a long time ago. We were all having a picnic in the forest, to celebrate. Your parents had finally found a home of their own, and were on their way there."

"What about me?" asked Mona. "Was I there?"

"Yes," said Strawberry, with a smile. "You were such a cute little mouseling."

Mona tried to remember. A basket, not like the one at the Heartwood, but small and made of sweetgrass. Seedcakes, warmed from the sun. The tickle of whiskers, and . . . a drop of rain?

"We were eating dessert when we saw storm

121

clouds gathering, darkening the sky," continued Strawberry. "I invited you all back to the Inn Between. It wasn't far away, but your parents wanted to reach their new home. They'd infringed upon hotels enough, they said. I told them that was ridiculous—that the Inn Between was always open to them. Your mother—she was . . ."

"She was family," finished Mona.

"Exactly," said Strawberry. "But she wouldn't listen. They were too determined to get to their new house. I should have insisted. I could have gone after them. But I didn't. I was already back at the Inn Between when the storm started."

"That was *the* storm," whispered Mona.

Strawberry added, "Now you see why I've been afraid to tell you." Her eyes moistened.

"I should have done something. I've always blamed myself."

Mona shook her head. "Don't." She would always miss her parents, but it wasn't Strawberry's fault.

Strawberry smiled, though it was tinged with sadness. "You are as sweet as sugar—but with a dash of spice." She handed the necklace back to Mona. "Now I must leave and let you rest."

She gave Mona a tight hug and a kiss on the forehead, and left.

The bed was very soft, but it wasn't her feather mattress. Mona tossed and turned, and so did her thoughts, from her parents to the Heartwood and back again. If only her parents had stayed at the Inn Between, they would have been safe. . . . At least everyone from the Heartwood was safe. Tilly and Henry must be settled in at Hood's by now.

How far away they felt! Mona remembered the seedcake. Would she *ever* get a chance to "Have at Hi" with her friend?

She sat up and pulled the bundle out of her pocket, then unwrapped it carefully. *Oh no!* Somewhere along her journey the piece of seedcake had gotten crushed. It was just seeds now. This was a sign for certain—a bad one. Still, she wrapped it up again and put it in her pocket, and lay back against the pillows. She felt her eyes filling up with tears, and closed them before any could spill out. She didn't want to cry.

At last Mona fell asleep, but her dreams were filled with floods that turned into flames. Closer, closer they came, until she could feel the heat on her fur. She woke up with a start. Her heart pounded. Where was she?

This wasn't the Heartwood. . . .

She looked frantically around. Of course. She

was at the Inn Between. The Heartwood . . . her home . . . it would soon be gone. Burned into nothing but a memory. She hated the fire. She hated it so much. Her throat felt tight, her mouth dry.

She checked the thimble on the nightstand, but it was empty. She needed some more tea.

Mona got up and tiptoed out of the room. The lights in the hallway were dim, and all was quiet. *Everyone must be asleep*, she thought. She didn't want to wake Strawberry. And besides, she didn't know where her room was, anyway. She would find the kitchen herself.

Down the hall she padded, unsure of which way to go. Down another, dark and hung with pictures of all the famous mice who had stayed there. Where would the kitchen be?

It was her nose that found it, a room that smelled of cheese and cinnamon, at the end of a half-hidden hall. The door was open, and Mona peeked in.

A long table was set up, with benches around it. Bowls and plates were laid out, ready for breakfast. There was even a chair positioned at one end. It was just like at the Heartwood . . . except everything was the perfect size for a mouse. For her. It should have felt right, but somehow it seemed much, much too small.

Against one wall were big buckets of crumbs, each labeled. She read a few: FROM THE FLOOR, FROM THE TABLE, FROM THE SOFA. One was even marked QUESTIONABLE. Strawberry had told her that the mice collected all their food from upstairs.

Where would the tea be? Mona was about to search the counters when she heard a voice.

"It's so, so sad. . . ."

The voice grew louder and was joined by the

sound of footsteps and a strange scratching. Mona ducked behind one of the buckets.

She peeked around the side and saw a soft glow. A firefly and the cricket, James, were pulling a basket. Inside was a cracker as big as Mona.

"You saw her, didn't you? She's such a little thing, for a mouse . . ." said the firefly. They began crumbling up the cracker and putting the pieces in the bucket at the far end.

"Hardly big enough to take on owls . . ." agreed James.

"Or wolves," said the firefly.

They were talking about her!

"Remember," said James, "don't say anything to the mouseling when she wakes up. Grandma Gooseberry doesn't want to worry her any more than she has already." Worry her? What did he mean?

The next moment, Mona found out.

The firefly's light flickered. "I do hope that hummingbird finds the owner. He wasn't at the Beaver Lodge. That's where everyone in the forest has gone now, since the water will keep them safe. So where else could he be?"

"It was silly to think he would have come here," said James. "Imagine a badger staying at the Inn Between!"

Mona stifled a gasp. Mr. Heartwood?!

The firefly crumbled the last bit of the cracker. "Come on, we have more to bring downstairs. The mice found a whole wedge of cheese under the armchair in the Big Library." They left, pulling the empty basket behind them.

Mona stood up slowly. She could hardly believe her ears. Mr. Heartwood was missing? She'd thought everyone was safe. Her whiskers trembled with worry. Where could he be?

Except for the Beaver Lodge, Mona couldn't remember him going anywhere. He was always at the Heartwood. He had still been there when the rest of the staff left. And he had been wearing boots and gloves, not his usual top hat and tie. Mona hadn't thought anything of it at the time. But now it seemed strange. As strange as what Grandma Gooseberry had said earlier about buckets of water and a trench. They hadn't dug a trench. They hadn't put out buckets of water. . . . Unless . . .

Unless Mr. Heartwood had!

Harmony couldn't find Mr. Heartwood for one simple reason. Mr. Heartwood had never left!

As soon as Mona thought it, she knew it was true, from deep in her heart to the tips of her whiskers.

What was he thinking? Mr. Heartwood would never be able to fight the whole fire himself! If it could jump over a huge patch of rocky ground, a trench and some buckets of water wouldn't stop it.

She rushed out of the kitchen.

Should she go find Strawberry? But what could Strawberry do? Besides, what if Strawberry stopped her? She had tried to stop her from helping Blaze—and that was just a baby fox. This was a forest fire. Strawberry *would* stop her to keep her safe. But Mona'd be safe. She'd turn back if she actually saw flames. Would Strawberry understand that?

Mona found her way back to the lobby. She

searched the desktop, looking for something to write on. There was a vase of flowers, a check-in book, and some hotel stationary with *IB* in swirly letters. She grabbed a pencil.

Dear Strawberry,

I have gone back to the Heartwood. Mr Heartwood is in danger! Please understand.

How to end it? How to show how much she cared about Strawberry, and how grateful she was for all her aunt had done? How much she wished the timing had been different?

She drew a little heart.

Beside it she wrote:

♡ Your niece, Mona

Home Again

Mona had scurried before—but never so quickly as this. She slid down the drainpipe and ran through the grasses. She reached the enormous river of stones and was halfway across when she felt the ground under her paws shudder, almost knocking her down. But Mona was good at balancing—all mice were—and she managed to right herself and dash across to safety.

Just in time—*VRRRROOOM!*

Her whole body shook. What was that? Mona turned to look, but whatever it was had disappeared. All that remained was a smell that made

her nose sting. Even though her legs were trembling, she knew she had to keep going.

With every step, she wished with all her might that she would make it in time. Soon, she came to the signs at the edge of the forest.

DANGER

The arrow pointed like a claw to Fernwood Forest. Not to the path Mona and Strawberry had taken. To a much larger path to the left.

What had Strawberry said? *Not that way. . . . It might get us there in half the time, but it's more likely we'll get eaten.*

The journey from the Heartwood to the Inn Between had taken Strawberry and her a full day—maybe half a night, too. She didn't have that much time. Mona had no choice. She thought of Mr. Heartwood and followed the DANGER sign.

The ground leading to the trail was trampled and easy to travel. Too easy. There were no bushes or brambles to hide under. Her fur stood on end

as she stepped between the twisted trunks of two dead trees and onto the trail itself. The tracks scarring the earth were triple her size. The air stank with the smell of smoke and the foul breath of wolves and owls. When she saw an owl pellet, a ball of fur and bones, she squeaked in fear, but she didn't stop.

Not until she heard voices up ahead.

"This way, Wince!"

"I hear you, Gnarl!"

She knew these voices, from months ago. These were the same wolves that had threatened the Heartwood in the fall. The sound of panting and paws thudding the earth came closer and closer.

Mona froze, expecting the worst.

But the wolves passed right by her! Gnarl and Wince, and a pack of others, including pups. Their fur was matted and streaked with soot. Their yellow eyes glittered with panic.

These wolves were frightened! They didn't even notice her as they ran. And strangest of all, every instinct in Mona told her to turn around and join them.

But she didn't. She scurried on.

She saw things she'd never imagined. A weasel slinking beside a family of squirrels. A hawk swooping down—not to attack, but only to cry, "Fly! Fly away!" The whole forest was upside down.

And then, the impossible—from the sky, through the trees, fell snow. Snow in the summer!

But it didn't glitter like snow, like stars. It fell dull and thick and powdery.

Not snow. Ash.

Falling on her fur, in big clumps, melting gray into brown. Though it didn't whip at her whiskers or sting her nose with cold like the blizzard in the winter, it was a hundred times worse.

How much farther could she go? She could feel the heat now, and the smoke, thick in her throat. She'd promised herself she'd stay safe—and if ash was falling like this . . .

The fire was close.

But so was the Heartwood!

Mona rounded a bend in the path, and there was the stream bank, dry and sandy. There was the moss, tucked and trimmed just so. And there was the tree!

The fire hadn't reached it yet!

It rose up, tall as ever. But majestic? No. Its golden-green crown was tarnished gray with ash.

 136

And its branches looked smaller, like someone had trimmed off their twigs. A dry trench ringed its base. Mr. Heartwood must have dug it, and filled the water buckets that circled the trunk. But no lights shone from any of the rooms.

It didn't look like a glorious, grand hotel.

Only a big old oak tree.

Mona felt tears prick at her eyes, though not from the smoke. She could see well enough. Well enough for her heart to break.

Except . . . there . . . on the door. The heart her father had carved. Mona's own heart took courage as she scrambled across the trench and pressed it.

With a creak, the door swung open, as it had a hundred, a thousand times before. And, like *she* had a hundred, a thousand times before, Mona stepped inside.

The lobby was dark and quiet. Too quiet. Mona could hear her own heart beating. And the faint tinkling of the room keys as she shut the door. They dangled from their hooks behind the front desk . . . every single one of them. The twig furniture was still stacked to the side from the picnic, the fireplace mantel bare of decorations. Only the wedding picture hung on the wall, the one of all the staff together. How long ago that seemed.

Mona shivered.

"Mr. Heartwood! Mr. Heartwood!" she cried. Her voice echoed.

No one replied.

She checked his office. It was empty. So were the ballroom and the dining room. Not just of guests, but of the things that made the Heartwood feel like home: The buttery smell of seedcakes and the rich nuttiness of acorn soufflé. The sound of chattering and of song. . . .

"Mr. Heartwood!" she cried again.

Mr. Heartwood, Mr. Heartwood . . . the tree called back.

Still no one answered.

Mr. Heartwood wasn't in the kitchen, either.

She checked all the rooms. . . . Where else could he be?

Of course! She hadn't checked *his*.

Mr. Heartwood's suite was the only one Mona had never been in. Nor had Tilly, as far as she knew.

 139

Mona scurried down the stairs. Down past the kitchen and the staff rooms, past the hibernation suites. Down, in the deep, deep dirt. It was cooler here, but it still wasn't safe. Fire could even spread to roots. She had to hurry.

At last, the staircase ended—at a large wooden door. It was open.

"Mr. Heartwood?" she tried to call, but her voice came out as a whisper.

She stepped inside. Mona had always imagined Mr. Heartwood lived in a suite grander than the penthouse. But this was a single humble room, centered around the main root of the tree, the heart of the oak itself. There was a desk, and a small shelf filled with books, and there, on the other side, sitting on a simple bed of dried grasses, was the badger.

He was wearing his boots and his patched vest, but his gloves lay beside him. He stared down at his paws, which were all bandaged up, clumsily

wrapped in two white pillowcases, like the one she had used for Blaze.

He was hurt. It must have been from all the digging.

"Mr. Heartwood . . . ?" she said softly.

The badger jumped. Upon seeing Mona, he wiped his eyes with one bandaged paw. He had been crying!

But when his gaze met Mona's his eyes flashed fiercely. His whiskers bristled.

"Miss Mouse!" he growled, standing up.

"It's okay, Mr. Heartwood," said Mona.

"No, no!" He shook his head. "You can't be

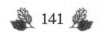

here. Begone with you, disappear!" His eyes widened and his whiskers stuck out straight, like quills. "You should be at the Inn Between, safe!"

"I'm here to . . . to help you," said Mona, suddenly feeling like everything was going wrong.

"Help? I don't need your help!" growled the badger.

"But, Mr. Heartwood . . . the fire is coming," Mona insisted.

"EXACTLY!" he growled, even louder this time. "Which is why you must go! At once!"

"But . . . you have to come with me. . . ."

Mr. Heartwood shook his head. "I can't leave, but leave *you* must."

Mona stumbled back in alarm. She had only thought about getting *to* Mr. Heartwood. She had never thought what might happen if he didn't want to go.

Mr. Heartwood strode forward, practically pushing her out of his suite and up the stairs.

"B-but . . ." she stammered.

Mr. Heartwood wasn't listening. Up the stairs, across the lobby, he directed her, right to the front door.

"Mr. Heartwood! Please!"

The great badger shook his head and opened the door, letting in a waft of smoke.

"Miss Mouse—Mona," he said, with a cough, "you have to understand. I must protect this hotel—for Mr. and Mrs. Higgins, for Gilles, for Tilly, Henry, for you . . ."

Mona turned to face him, and caught a glimpse of the wedding portrait, hanging on the wall. Everyone together, with Mr. Heartwood at the center. Not gathered around the tree, but around him. . . . She had been wrong before. The Heartwood wouldn't be gone—but it *was* in danger.

"I need to stay with my hotel," he said.

"But, Mr. Heartwood, you ARE the hotel!" Mona burst out. "You want to save the Heartwood?

Well, then you have to save yourself. Come on," she said. She stepped outside, the smoke thick and heavy all around her. It was hard to see, hard to breathe. "I love this tree. I love it so much. Almost as much as you do. But you've done everything you can to protect it. It's up to the tree now." The smoke got the better of her. She ended up doubled over in a fit of coughing. When she stood up again, the door was closed.

Had Mr. Heartwood heard anything she had said?

She didn't know. She did know she was no longer safe. She had to go.

And then . . .

The door opened.

There, through the smoke, strode the great badger.

14

FACING FIRE

In one bandaged paw, he held a small suitcase. "Miss Mouse . . ."

"Oh, Mr. Heartwood!" Mona threw her paws around him.

"Thank you, little one," he said in a croak, patting her on the head. "Now, we must get to the stream bank. It will lead us to the Lodge."

The smoke was thicker than ever now. Mona's nose stung, and she thought about Henry's story of the onions and how he had protected himself from the smell. She clutched her apron tightly over her face, keeping only her eyes free, following closely behind Mr. Heartwood. It was difficult to see, and she could barely make out where they were going. Suddenly Mr. Heartwood stopped.

They were at the trench.

Beyond, the forest was ablaze. Fearsome sparks flew from branches. Mona could hear the trees crying out in crackles. She stumbled back in shock. Mr. Heartwood reached for her.

"This way!" he said, guiding her. "Perhaps we can get through around the back."

They rushed behind the Heartwood. But the fire burned beyond the trench there, too. They were surrounded.

"We waited too long. . . . It's all my fault!" Mr. Heartwood cried.

Mona opened her mouth to reassure him, but no sound came out.

All the months at the Heartwood, all the adventures, all the stories, swirled inside her head. There was no story to save them now.

Or was there? "The tunnel! Mr. Heartwood, the Tunnel of Two Hearts!" Her words were muffled by her apron, but Mr. Heartwood must have heard her, for he headed to the garden, his suitcase nearly slipping from his paws more than once.

Mr. Higgins had dug the tunnel starting from the garden. It led to the stream. But where was the entrance?

Mr. Heartwood knew. He pushed back the peppermint plants, which were always overgrown, and now Mona saw why. There in the ground was a hole, covered with a board.

Mr. Heartwood moved the board aside. "Go!" he cried.

Mona slipped in, tumbling down, down into the dry dirt. Mr. Heartwood followed. The deeper

they went, the cooler it
was, and the soil turned
damp and smelled faintly
of hedgehog. It was too dark to see
anything. Were they passing
under the flames? Would
the roots burst into
fire? Or would the tun-
nel take them to safety?

At last, they climbed up,
up, up.

The dirt turned dry again.
They were almost there.
Mona's heart pounded.
She could see light,
hazy light, but no
flames.

POOF! She emerged in a cloud of dust.

The tunnel had worked! There, just beyond
them, was the streambed. There was no time to

catch her breath. Glancing back, Mona could see the fire was still coming, sparking and snapping behind them. Mr. Heartwood emerged from the tunnel, covered in dirt. One bandage was filthy and falling off. In his other paw, he still clutched his suitcase. He used it to point to the stream bank.

They ran down the bank onto the dry rocks and sand below.

"My suitcase!" coughed Mr. Heartwood. He'd dropped it, and it was rolling down the streambed, disappearing into smoke. He began after it, clumsily but urgently.

"I'll get it!" cried Mona. "Mr. Heartwood, just go!"

She didn't wait for him to answer.

The suitcase rolled and rolled, at last stopping between two rocks. She scurried to get it, but it was stuck. No matter how hard she pulled and tugged, it wouldn't come free. *I have to leave it*, she thought, when . . .

POP! Out it tumbled—and she tumbled with it. When she righted herself, she could no longer see Mr. Heartwood.

Was that him, up ahead?

She stumbled forward, clutching the case.

THUMP! Something fell, landing right in front of her, shaking the ground.

Fire!

A burning branch had fallen into the streambed, blocking her way. Flames twirled and swirled in a dizzying dance.

Mona couldn't move, couldn't breathe, she was so scared.

There was no tricking fire. It wasn't a wolf or an owl, or even a snowstorm you could outwait. She thought she could, with the tunnel.

But she couldn't.

Usually, Mona was good at balancing, but

she felt faint. The suitcase was heavy. . . .

The fire crackled and spat, so close, so loud now. But over the noise, Mona thought she heard something else. No, it couldn't be.

And then . . .

First a trickle, spilling down the streambed. Not much, but enough. Enough to put out the flames. Then a *WHOOSH*, washing away the branch.

Water!

Cool, beautiful water.

It began to rush now, lifting Mona up until her paws could barely touch the bottom, about to carry her away, just like when the water had swept her up in the storm and carried her to the hotel so many seasons ago.

Frantically, she reached out for something to hold on to. But there was no root this time.

Except . . . there was a paw—*many* paws—pulling her up, up the bank on the other side of the stream.

"Mona! Mona!"

There was Strawberry, and Tilly, and Henry, Mr. and Mrs. Higgins, Gilles, and even Mr. Heartwood. Her friends, her family—all her family—there, coming for her.

She collapsed into them, hugging them, coughing, so happy, so glad that they were together again— with the water protecting them, flowing between them and the fire like a song, almost a rhyme:

Splish, splash, splish, splash,
Safe at last, safe at last.

An Unexpected Ending

"Mona!" cried Tilly and Strawberry, throwing their paws around her.

"Thank goodness you're safe, too," said Mrs. Higgins. Then she turned to Mr. Heartwood and scolded, "Georgie! What were you thinking?"

Mr. Heartwood stammered, "I—I'm sorry."

"Sorry?! No time for sorries," said Tilly. "We have to get out of here! The water's protecting us for now, but it'll run out soon."

There was no chance for Mona to ask why. Tilly grabbed her paw. "Hurry!"

Mona tried. But her legs wouldn't let her. She

couldn't hurry anywhere. She had been scurrying forever. She was so, so tired, it was hard to keep her eyes open.

An orange flame slid beside her. She blinked. More fire?! No, it was a fox. Blaze! What was he doing here? He crouched down, as though he wanted her to climb on.

His paw was no longer bandaged. . . . And her paws hurt, ached. . . . And her head spun from the heat. . . .

Before she could think, she clambered onto his back.

His fur was soft, soft as a featherbed, although a little full of ash. The last thing she heard before sinking into his fur, and into sleep, was Tilly's unmistakable huff. "Sure! *You* get a ride!"

When Mona woke up, she wasn't in a fancy bedroom under a quilt made of ribbons, or resting in the Heartwood penthouse. She wasn't in a bedroom at all.

She was lying on a bed of sticks, with the smoky sky as her ceiling. A few stars shone through a clear patch, and it felt like she could reach out and touch them.

For a moment, she thought she was on the stargazing balcony.

Then she looked around and saw other stick beds, some filled with sleeping animals. And there, at the edge of wherever she was, sat two squirrels and a mouse.

She pushed off a thin blanket made of bulrushes and stood up, wobbly. Stepping carefully because the floor—or was it a roof?—was slightly sloped, she made her way over to them.

"Tilly?" she started to say, but coughed instead.

"Mona!" Tilly exclaimed.

"There, there, sugar, sit down! Slowly, now."
Strawberry made room for Mona on her chair.
Gone were Strawberry's hat and her gloves. She
was streaked in soot and ash. Mona knew she must
be, too.

Below them was a pond—in the middle of
a meadow, ringed with willow trees. Instead of
water, most of the pond was filled with animals,
some sitting on stones, others standing or huddling
together.

Mona was sure she recognized a few. Was that
rabbit down there on that rock the Duchess? And
was that Francis the deer? She could make out
Blaze. But she was up higher than them all.

"Wh-where am I?" she stammered.

"The Beaver Lodge," said Tilly. "Or . . . what's
left of it. We came here with Hood when the fire
changed direction. Everyone did."

"There're no more rooms inside, so we've made
some on the roof," piped up Henry.

So it is a roof, thought Mona.

"It's the sun-basking balcony, for turtles," Henry went on. He pointed to the chair, which was made from thick lily pads stretched across a wooden frame. "This is for sun-basking. Isn't it neat? It's SO round, and even a bit bouncy!"

"Don't bounce, Henry," scolded Tilly. "You don't want to break anything! Right now the Lodge is for animals that are hurt, or breathed in too much smoke, or have nowhere else to go," she explained.

"But . . . I thought the Lodge would be under-water," Mona said, confused. "Isn't it a water hotel?"

Then she remembered the water, flowing down the streambed.

"There's no water left except in the luxury pool. That's where the water animals are staying," said Tilly. "When Strawberry came, we knew you and Mr. Heartwood were in trouble. Mr. Benjamin directed the water animals into the luxury pool, and had the rest of us break down the dam. He knew the stream flowed near the Heartwood. He hoped it would buy us some time to find you."

"Strawberry rode on Blaze!" said Henry.

"*Strawberry?*" Mona looked at the older mouse in disbelief.

"Yes," said Strawberry. "Your note . . . You should've waited. You should've woken me."

"I didn't know where your room was," said Mona. "And I thought you might . . ."

Strawberry took a deep breath. "Perhaps I would have stopped you. I don't know. By the time I got your note and left, the fire blocked my way to the Heartwood. I didn't know what to do . . . until . . . I saw a fox. I was so scared, but then he told me his name. It was Blaze. He thought I was you. He helped me. He took me to the Lodge. He's a good little pup, for a fox. That's when Benjamin came up with his plan."

"So the fire . . . ?" Mona hardly dared to ask.

"It's still burning," said Tilly.

Mona looked over at the forest. She couldn't see flames anymore. She had hoped maybe it was over, because the sky was clearing.

"But the wind's changed. The rain is coming! Any moment now!" said Henry excitedly. "I know because I am a groundhog guesser!"

"Henry!" said Tilly. "You are not. You've just made friends with them, that's all."

"If Harmony can be a messenger jay, why can't I be a groundhog guesser?"

"'Cause that's not the truth! You're a squirrel, that's why!" groaned Tilly. "And a bellhop, too!"

"Not anymore," said Henry, and there was silence.

"Tilly, do you mind giving Mona and me a moment alone?" said Strawberry at last. "Perhaps you and Henry can fetch more of those lily-pad puffs?"

"Urgh," groaned Henry. "Those are the worst!"

"But Henry, cupcake," said Strawberry, "you've eaten ten!"

"EXACTLY," groaned Henry, and bounded away, disappearing over the side of the Lodge. Tilly headed down the ladder after him.

She gave Mona a suspicious glance. Mona raised her eyebrows in answer. She still had to tell Tilly everything she'd learned at the Inn Between.

Just as she was thinking this, when Tilly had climbed down out of sight, Strawberry said, "There's something I must tell you, sugar." She took a deep breath. "Mona, I'm not your aunt."

SEEDS AND A SUITCASE

"What?" cried Mona in astonishment.

"WHAT?!" came a louder voice.

Tilly popped her head up over the side of the Lodge.

Strawberry sighed and motioned for Tilly to join them. "You might as well."

Tilly sheepishly sat down. "But the necklaces . . ." she said.

"And everything at the Inn Between," said Mona. "Didn't you know my mom?"

"Yes, of course. But I wasn't her sister."

Strawberry gazed at Tilly and Mona, both. "I was her best friend."

"Best friend?!" Tilly looked devastated.

Mona blinked. But . . . how could this be? Strawberry herself had told Mona she was her aunt. Or . . . had she? Mona had been so sure she knew Strawberry's secret, she hadn't let her finish what she was going to say.

"I met Madeline when we were only mouse-lings," explained Strawberry. "We played together all the time. Then, when she was old enough, she came to work at the Inn Between as a maid—like you at the Heartwood, Mona."

Strawberry pulled out her necklace. "This seed, it's very special. A sister seed. We may not have been born sisters, but we became them."

"But not *really*," said Tilly. "Not *truly*!"

"Why not?" said Mona slowly.

Tilly turned to her, in disbelief. "You have to

have the same parents, and, you know . . . there're rules!"

"So . . . you wouldn't give me a sister seed?" asked Mona.

"That's . . . that's different. You and me . . ." Tilly humphed. "Great! Next I'll be telling Henry he can be a groundhog guesser!"

But she was smiling. Mona, too.

A secret might not be told at the right time. It might not even be the secret you expect. But who decided what was right, anyway?

At that very moment, a cry came fast as a hum: "Rain-rain-rain!"

Maybe Tilly *would* have to let Henry be a groundhog guesser. He had predicted right!

Harmony came zipping over the pond. "It's-raining-over-Fernwood!" she cried. "It's-raining-over-Fernwood!"

When all was burned and ugly, the sky cried. *Rain!* It hadn't reached them yet, but it was falling on the fire. Harmony had brought good news at last. The *best* news.

Mona, Strawberry, and Tilly leapt up and hugged one another.

Everyone cheered—and then everyone danced!

A bear bobbed alongside bees. A fox and rabbit hopped together. Even Mr. Heartwood was dancing with Mr. Benjamin in a funny waltz that sent mud splattering, much to Henry's delight.

The pond had become a great ballroom. Frogs and crickets made up the band.

Mona, Tilly, and Strawberry hurried down to join the fun.

It felt like the entire forest was there. And they all wanted to talk and dance with Mona. Skim the snail, Hood the rat, the skunk couple the Sudsburys (who definitely must have sprayed in fright). Mona was extra glad when the rain began to fall while

she was talking to them, so she didn't have to keep plugging her nose.

In celebration, an otter in an apron appeared with lily-pad puffs for everyone, and Strawberry made a whole jug of lemongrass tea from the rainfall.

The drops fell, sweet and cool, and Mona closed her eyes and lifted her nose. They slipped down her whiskers and soaked into her fur.

"Mona?"

Mona opened her eyes to see Tilly holding half of a seedcake. The one they'd split in two. She hadn't eaten it.

But . . .

Mona reached into her apron pocket. She pulled out her bundle and unwrapped it. "Look," she said. "I'm so sorry, Till. I didn't mean to break it."

"It's okay," said Tilly. "I was thinking . . ." She held up the seedcake in the rain. "Maybe we don't want to eat them after all. . . . Maybe . . ." Tilly

166

let the rain dissolve her cake, washing it away, until there were only two seeds left.

Sister seeds. Their very own.

In the morning, it was different. Quiet. The fire was out, but what now? Everyone was scared to go back into the forest, scared to see what damage the fire had done. Including the staff of the Heartwood Hotel. Mona had tried not to think of the dear old tree. But now she couldn't help it.

Strawberry told her again the Inn Between was always open to her, and it was good to know she had a place where she would be welcomed. At the moment, though, she needed to stay with Tilly and Mr. Heartwood. "I understand, sugar," Strawberry said.

Mr. Heartwood gathered everyone together in the meadow beside the pond. The grass still sparkled from the rain. It was wet on Mona's paws, but she didn't mind. She stared off into the forest. The trees at the edge were green, but that was as far as she could see.

All was dark beyond them.

"Everything is going to be gone," said Mrs. Higgins, punctuating her sentence with a sneeze.

"The forest grows," Mr. Higgins replied reassuringly, handing her a handkerchief, which was really too muddy to be useful.

His words didn't reassure Gilles. "Five acorns," Gilles sputtered, flicking his tongue in and out. "That's what the Heartwood had. We'll never have another hotel like it."

"Or another tree," said Tilly. "Do you think, Mr. Heartwood, it could have . . ."

Mr. Heartwood took a deep breath. "It's hard to hope, but we'll have to see. No matter what, it was a special tree." He paused. "As for the hotel, as long as we are together and have this, we cannot go amiss."

He held up his suitcase. His paws were still

bandaged, but they were neatly wrapped now. "Thanks to Miss Mouse, for rescuing it for me." He gave her a deep nod. "I am more than grateful."

"A suitcase?" Henry wasn't impressed. "I've seen *lots* of suitcases. They're not so special."

"Shh! Something's in it, Henry," said Tilly.

But what? Mona held her breath as the badger undid the clasps.

He took out a large rolled-up piece of bark. Slowly, he unrolled it. WE LIVE BY "PROTECT AND RESPECT," NOT BY "TOOTH AND CLAW."

"Our sign!" cried Mrs. Higgins.

"Our sign?" Henry looked less than thrilled.

But Mona was. She beamed, and the sun did, too—shining on the sign, soft and gold, lighting up one word in particular. She'd never noticed it until now. The sign began with the word "we."

Of course it did.

She looked around at Tilly and Henry and everyone else.

WE LIVE BY "PROTECT AND RESPECT," NOT BY "TOOTH AND CLAW."

Summer would soon end. All the seasons would come and go. Leaves would bud and green, then crisp and fall. The sky would smile and cry, and so would she. But she would be okay.

She had a family. And as long as she was with them, she was home.

THE END

THE PINECONE PRESS: NEWS! NEWS! NEWS!
Grand Reopening of the Heartwood Hotel

Owner Mr. Heartwood is pleased to announce the grand reopening of the marvelous Heartwood Hotel. All are invited to join in a daylong celebration. Enjoy complimentary seedcakes and honeyed iced tea. Tour new features of the hotel, including the special circular pool for young ones and a luggage chute for quick checkouts.

Learn more about the Heartwood Hotel and its story from Mr. Heartwood himself and star employee Mona the mouse. This end-of-summer party is sure to please paws and antennae alike.

In the meantime, stay safe, eat in earnest, and be happy . . . no matter where you may be! —Juniper Jones, *Pinecone Press* reporter

All proceeds from the first week's bookings will be going to FeRR (Fernwood Replanters and Rebuilders).

IN OTHER NEWS: See page 3 for a five-acorn review of the Inn Between—also taking in homeless animals during this time of need!